Praise for Jason White

"Mr. White masterfully weaves together tales of terror rife with horrifying images that linger long after the story is over. This is a writer to be watched." —*Sèphera Girón, author of House of Pain, The Narcissist's BLT, and The Witch's Field*

"I've seen a lot of attempts to retell Poe, too, and this is probably the best. (As a long time fan, I have to at least reserve some doubt in favor of Clive Barker's 'New Murders in the Rue Morgue," but there I go digressing again.) What I love most about this story is that while it remains reasonably true to the original, Jason's managed to keep his own voice throughout. Surprising, actually, how well his natural voice blends with Poe's story. Also surprising how well the story lends itself to a modern retelling." —*Inanna Gabriel, Title Goes Here: Magazine and author of Act Four Scene Three*

"[Chemical Burn] is best taken with a toke and a drink, followed by another toke. Its psychedelic nature begs for you to join in its quest for spiritual logic and, dare I say, dominance." —*C . Bryan Brown, Title Goes Here: Magazine*

Isolation

Stories By

Jason White

Darkly Horrific Books

ISBN-13: 978-0987856449
ISBN-10: 0987856448

Edited by Diana Cox
Cover art © Ronnell D. Porter

Dedicated to Jen, who puts up with my shit and still claims to love me.

Contents

"Room 118" originally appeared in The Harrow, Vol 9, No 11.

"Chemical Burn" originally appeared in Title Goes Here: Magazine Issue 4.

"Divorce and the Black Cat" originally appeared in Title Goes Here: Magazine, Web Eition 1.8.

"The Seminary" originally appeared in a slightly different version in the Heavy Metal Horror anthology by Rymfire eBooks.

"House of Coal" originally appeared nanobison, issue number 9.

"The Serpent's Son" originally appeared in The Harrow Vol 11, No 2.

"Isolation" originally appeared in the Revenant anthology by Rymfire eBooks.

"Surviving the Fittest" originally appeared in Book of the Dead Volume 4: Dead Rising by Living Dead Press.

"The Witch at Midnight" originally appeared in the Etched Offerings anthology by Misanthrope Press.

Acknowledgements

This collection would not be possible if it were not for the people listed here. Each one helped in one way or another as I traveled this long and mostly frustrating journey: Sèphera Girón for the kind words, the lessons, and the friendship; Michael Rowe for doing much more than what was needed; Michael Colangelo for the great conversations over beer and cigarettes, also for being the first to publish a story of mine with money involved; Dru Pagliassotti for paying me said money; Inanna Gabriel and C. Bryan Brown for all the kind words and incredible support; Griffin Hayes for the encouragement and a guest spot on his blog. Thanks also go to Anthony Giangregorio, Armand Rosamilia, Doug Helbling, Jeffrey Conolly, and Aldo Calcagno.

I'd also like to thank my mother, Sharyn Eby, for having the surgery in order to get pregnant with me along with her continual support throughout my life; Jennifer Barnes and the Barnes family for their support and for buying the magazines and anthologies in which my work appeared; Richard Somers for the eyes and the insane conversations; Cora Saint Laurent who, in the beginning of the journey, pushed me to write every day; my grade ten and eleven English teacher, Mr. Fogg, for telling me that I had talent.

Last, but not least, I thank Tressa Francher, Danielle Hill, Eileen Carr Rutter, Marc-antoine, Thoa Sey, Jennifer Byrkit, and everyone at the GoodReads forum, Horror Aficionados, for their friendship and their support.

Isolation

There was something about the cottage that didn't sit well in Kate's stomach. Perhaps it was the size. *Not really a cottage*, she thought, *but an old house out here in the middle of nowhere, surrounded by an army of trees and a nation of insects*. She cursed the mosquitoes and swiped a hand at their incessant buzzing around her ears. Before her, the cottage stood with two-floors complete with a balcony on the second story. Above that, just beneath the triangular roof, there was a circular window to what Kate supposed was the attic.

"You'll be surprised by its size," Kate's mother had told her before she left. "But don't let its age discourage you. It's kept up very well. Mr. Barker prepares it for winter every year. He also works on it during the summer months, making sure it doesn't fall down in case I ever decide to use it."

Kate wondered what Kevin would make of the place. The house was of the sort he would have loved, somewhat large and full of mysteries, and if he had known of its existence.... She pushed the thought from her mind, refusing to give in to guilt or think of the emptiness Kevin had once filled. She had traveled ten hours to get here, after all, to get away, refresh her batteries, and to "Forget the pain" as her mother had said.

But still, standing alone by her SUV, two suitcases sitting at her feet, something wiggled in the pit of her stomach as her eyes soaked in the image before her. It was as though she had dreamed of the place in some long forgotten nightmare. *Cell memory*, she considered, remembering stories of her great-aunt who had apparently lived out here alone for a time, before killing herself. The house was built by Kate's great-grandfather over a hundred years ago, and was meant for family vacations back when the Hillside's had money to throw around. Nobody but her great-aunt Sylvia, however, had actually lived in the place.

To Kate, the family cottage looked like nothing more than an old, haunted house.

She wondered how long it had been since anyone had stayed here. Years? Decades? Probably the latter, but it no longer mattered. Her eyes stung from the long drive, her muscles and joints ached, and all she wanted to do was to unpack and crawl into bed, if there was one, and fall into a deep sleep. She picked up her bags and considered one last time hopping into the SUV, finding a motel and crashing before heading back home. She would have done so if the thought of spending one minute longer inside the vehicle didn't make her want to scream. It outweighed the unease the cottage summoned. So Kate stumbled up the porch steps, opened the door, and went inside.

She reached over and flicked the switch beside the front door, and to her surprise, soft orange light illuminated the front foyer. She could smell old, dried-out wood, the years of dust that had recently covered everything. To her left was the lounge room with a yellowish couch and chair, both very ancient by the looks of them and covered with plastic. To her right, the dinning room, the table and chairs all stained nearly black. Ahead was a corridor that Kate supposed lead to the kitchen. All these she ignored as she headed up the stairs.

Kevin would have loved this house.

Upstairs, there were three bedrooms. Only one had a bed, located at the front of the house. The master bedroom, and it was here where she unpacked her clothes and changed into her pajamas. Before crawling into bed as she had planned, she opened the screen door to the balcony and stood there, letting the cool breeze wash over and ease frayed nerves. The fresh air was inviting with its smells of wilderness. She stepped outside, the maple and pine and spruce of the forest standing before her like tall soldiers, awaiting her command. They would watch over and protected her in this isolation, this long reprieve from a life that had changed so suddenly, so drastically. Stepping back inside, she crawled into the king-size bed, happy that the sheets smelled of fabric softener rather than the dust and mold she feared.

She would phone her mother and thank her for this wonderful gift later. Now her eyelids hung heavy, and she closed them, letting the darkness seduce her into oblivion.

* * *

Kate awoke to moonlight with the dream memory of cold, hard fingers grasping at her wrists. As the dream faded, she sat up and realized she wasn't alone.

Off in the distance, a wolf bayed at the moon. Other wolves answered the call, and Kate's heart fluttered at the sound of it. She was a city girl used to the sounds of emergency vehicle sirens, not this wildness. Much closer than the baying wolves, almost as an undercurrent to the night song, was a low and constant hum. Growling, she realized, cocking her head. Coming from the front yard.

But it was the womanly silhouette standing out on the balcony that made her heart pound ice through her bloodstream. Female in its hourglass shape, with two thin arms hanging loosely at her sides, its head was disfigured with wisps and curls of shadow. Kate could not tell if the apparition was looking at her or down on the front yard.

She wondered if Mr. Barker had come to visit during her slumber, and that was his wife standing out there, so motionless and silent.

"Hel—Hello?"

The silhouette moved. Kate curled her knees up to her chest, her back pressing painfully against the bed's headboard. The figure turned around and, peering inside with a quizzical tilt to its upper body, entered the bedroom. Kate's breath turned to mist before her eyes. Goose bumps trailed up her arms. She reached to her right, her hand moving along the wall with frantic motions. When her hand found the plastic switch, yellow light filled the room, blinding her.

Her breath caught in her lungs, and through blurred vision that cleared too quickly, she took in the sight before her. A woman it indeed was, but Kate quickly dismissed the idea that this was Mr. Barker's wife. She wore a wedding dress that fanned out at the hips and ran down to her toes, her veil up to cover her hair. The exposed skin of her arms and face was smooth and grey, ageless. Her eyes were large and silver. She stood just inside the bedroom, her upper body tilted to the side as though that was her normal posture. She stared down at Kate, her grey lips parted into an O. The woman raised her eyebrows, and then she spoke.

"You hold the same pain as I," she said.

Kate screamed, and she found herself up on her feet, running away from the woman, out of the bedroom and down the stairs. The decision to leave, in fact, did not occur to her until she was half-way to the front door. She could get Mr. Barker to mail her things to her later, but for now, she had to get *out*.

She stopped after opening the front door. When she had gone to bed, she had unintentionally left the front foyer light on. The light switch had also turned on the front porch light, and through its orange-yellow glare, beasts of the like she'd never before seen stood blocking her way.

Doglike, they walked on four legs, curled their chops to snarl at her as drool pooled down on the ground by their feet. Their bodies, however, looked sculpted from clay by some insane artist. Large, like lions, but hairless, their brown skin was splotched with pink. The muscles of the beasts' legs and backs and necks bulged into massive dunes of flesh. They smelled strongly of the fertilizer in the cornfields Kate had driven by on her way here. Their eyes glowed in the same silver as the woman upstairs, and atop their ears was the only fur Kate could find in her panicked study. The fur, more like gelled hair, stood up on end, making the creatures' ears seem like horns. Kate stopped counting them at ten; they filled the front yard, sat upon her SUV like cats lazily soaking in the moonlight.

There was no leaving. Not tonight.

"These are my pets," the strange woman's whispery voice spoke from behind her. A breeze touched the hair over Kate's ears, smelling of rotted meat. Kate let out a soundless scream, her vision of the beasts blurring with tears.

"They came to me when poor Henry failed to return to me from fighting in some silly war. He brought his friends, and they keep coming. They are my companions now, my friends, and they are best viewed without this tasteless light."

The comfort of the light disappeared, and in the darkness, the creatures glowed with the moonlight, their eyes like massive disks of shinning nickel. They growled at her presence, licking their chops, the ones before the porch pacing back and forth, back and forth, those large eyes never once leaving hers. And she felt her knees buckle, the world's gravity suddenly too heavy for her to remain standing, and Kate fell onto the hardwood, all sights and smells swallowed into an empty abyss of blessed darkness.

* * *

"The things they make men do these days. My poor Henry didn't want to go to war. He wanted to stay here, with me. But they made him go anyway."

The plastic covering beneath Kate caused her skin to perspire. Someone or some*thing* had dragged her away from the front door, away from salvation. Kate opened her eyes. Bathed in silver, the strange woman sat upon the chair, slumped over Kate, speaking to her with those wide, almost amused eyes.

But a strange woman she was not. Her mother had shown her pictures of her great-aunt Sylvia many times before, enough for her to recognize the woman right away if circumstances had been normal. Here at the cottage, however, nothing was normal. From the house called a cottage to the caretaker never seen, from the apparition of her long dead great-aunt to the doglike creatures waiting to chew on her bones outside. *Oh God*, she thought, *nothing here is normal*.

"When I close my eyes, I can see them," Aunt Sylvia continued. "Rows upon rows of dead men, lying in a field a million miles away from home. They fight like animals, you know. You can't lie to me, my dear, so don't try. I know you've seen the same things as I have when you close your eyes. Your visit to me was no mistake. You belong here. The fact that my pets didn't devour you whole is evidence enough.

"Yes, I could see it in you when I first saw you. Your own husband, far, far away, lying on a road with his friends, his comrades, their bodies burned, their limbs torn free from their bodies. He didn't even have the chance to think of you one last time before the explosion.

"The silly things men are sent to do these days."

Kevin.

Tears welled in Kate's eyes. The casket had remained closed for the funeral, of course, the Canadian flag draped over it as though it were something to be proud of, this pointless death, these military men and women Kevin had never known showing blank, indifferent faces as they folded and then handed the flag to Kate. It had made her guts twist then, as it did so now.

"I'll only be half a year in Afghanistan," Kevin had said. "I'll be home before you know it. I promise."

Lies! All of it lies.

"Yes," her great-aunt Sylvia said. "It is only right for you to feel this way." She shifted position upon her seat, her porcelain face darkening as her own haunts and rages took over. From outside, the doglike creatures howled, sounding almost like a chorus of human grief. Like a song, a true and honest requiem, it crawled deep into Kate's mind, her heart. The tears within her eyes dried, stinging in their departure.

When Sylvia spoke again, her voice was loud and cold. She looked out the window, from where the hounds continued to sing. "Their wounds only fester here, growing puss where blood should be. My pets, my loved ones, my only company. You will join us, child, and never again shall we be alone."

Sylvia's image reflected too well all the emotions Kate had felt since receiving notice of her husband's death and she sat up, her head swimming with tiny stars sparkling in her vision. Aunt Sylvia remained where she was, only her eyes moved as they followed Kate. Where there had been a look of permanent amusement, her expression was now sour—her pouting lips turned black, her eyebrows heavy at the center with patches of black beneath the eyes. She looked up at her with naked hate, a rage that only so many years alone with only the hounds of her thoughts for company could hone to such deadliness. This exact face existed within Kate herself as well. She could see its likeness every time she closed her eyes.

Such a face only wanted seclusion from the outside world.

Like the isolation I desire.

"Yes, words and appearances can be deceiving," her great-aunt Sylvia snarled. When she smiled, the howling from outside stopped as though the hounds had never existed. But Aunt Sylvia remained the same.

Raising a grey finger that was black at its tip, as though she had submerged it into an inkwell, she stood and motioned for Kate to follow.

"I want to show you something," she said.

Kate followed her up the stairs, marveling at how real and solid the apparition looked in her hesitant, slow steps. *Perhaps Sylvia hadn't died*, Kate thought. *Perhaps she had lived and nobody knew any better of it*. But that didn't explain the hounds, nor Sylvia's inhuman complexion that changed with her moods. Still, Kate followed as Aunt Sylvia lowered the steps from the ceiling of the second floor that led up to the attic, trying to make sense of what her eyes and ears told her was real.

Dust rained down, coating Kate's hair and shoulders like snow. Fighting the urge to sneeze, she rubbed her nose and then followed her aunt up the steps, which creaked and groaned only under her weight, but not Sylvia's. From above, the faint glow of a fire illuminated the attic ceiling. Candles, she realized entering the attic. The candles rested on the many piles of boxes and chests that filled the room, so many candles that sweat beaded upon Kate's forehead and upper lip.

The body captured all of Kate's attention, however. She hung from a noose strung around the attic's middle rafter, wearing the same ancient wedding dress as her Aunt Sylvia. But the body was decomposed, the fabric of the dress rotted, and only a forensic unit would be able to identify the remains.

"Take a close look," Aunt Sylvia said. "This is where bitterness ends up."

Kate's stomach churned as blood drained from her face. From the hanging woman's chest, through the fabric and skin that no longer existed, through a ribcage lined with spider webs and dust, sat a heart, black and shriveled in the candlelight. Its oval and thin flesh expanded, as though breathing, then deflated. It was beating, Kate realized, beating an odd and sickly rhythm that drummed in her ears—*ba doom ... da ba doom*—and Kate screamed.

The apparition screamed also, her voice inhuman, a high-pitched squeal that drowned out all other noise and sent Kate to her knees, her hands at her ears. Wind blew within the attic, blowing out the candles, and then all was silent.

Silent, save for the palpitating beat of the withered heart. Aunt Sylvia's heart, Kate knew.

Kate crawled towards the soft light of the attic entry, using the light from the opened bedroom doorway below as a beacon. She slipped on the steps leading down onto the second floor and landed hard on her backside. There she remained, staring up at the black hole that was the attic above.

I'm losing my mind, she thought, but her mind and body were too exhausted to respond. As her eyes grew heavy, her heartbeat slowed ... and slowed until it matched the irregular rhythm that now beat within her ear canals.

Ba doom ... da ba doom.

And in the distance, a lone wolf howled a lullaby into the night sky.

* * *

Kate woke to sunlight that shone through the hallway with golden brilliance. She woke to a stiff back and aching legs, the strong smells of the chemical Mr. Barker had used on the carpets. She woke to the thought that it would be rational, sane, if she were to get up and leave. Even if she had to walk all the way back to the main road, leaving this place behind was the only sane thing any sane person would do.

The dropdown stairs leading to the attic remained where they were from last night, but Kate ignored it as she got up and headed to the master bedroom. Here, she turned off the light and began packing her clothes. While doing so, she forced herself not to think of the things that had happened last night. Whether she had imagined it, dreamed it, hallucinated it, or it had really happened didn't matter. She would forget. She would cram the memory down into the moldy basement of her mind, lock the door, and swallow the bloody key.

Instead, she focused on the pain each step caused from her fall last night. She must have twisted her ankle. Inspecting it, she noticed that it was swollen and colored in blues, reds, blacks, and greens. She also focused on the pain of having lost her husband, thinking of how it felt to have his arms around her, his lips against hers, how it would feel if he were to appear right now as if he had never joined the military and this was nothing but a vacation at its end.

All packed, she hobbled down to the first floor and out the front door. She tossed the suitcases into the SUV's backseat. In the driver's seat, she turned the engine over. But then she paused. The house stood before her like some lost relic, a tomb holding within its walls the secrets of surviving tragedy and the isolation it brings. She wondered idly what the house would look like with a fresh coat of paint, before considering the events of last night. Had the ghost of her great-aunt Sylvia truly come to her amongst a pack of hounds? The thought seemed ludicrous out here in the sunlight, but she couldn't very well leave without finding some evidence to the contrary. In all her life, Kate had never once seen a ghost. Up and until her husband died, she had lived a normal, average life. Her losing her mind after arriving here just didn't make sense.

Kate looked up at the circular window near the top of the house.

The attic window.

She had to know. And there was only one way to find out.

* * *

The attic entrance gaped at her from above, a giant, toothless mouth, ever hungry yet patient. She took the steps slowly, using her bad foot as an anchor to make it up to the next rung, the strength of her arms to help pull herself up. The wood creaked beneath her weight, and more than once she feared the steps would break and send her back down to the floor, but soon enough she was sitting on the attic floor, looking down at the patterned carpet below her. For a long moment she sat there, not wanting to look up, knowing deep within herself that there was nothing there, that there had never been anything there.

And if there was, then she'd take something with her, a piece of clothing, jewelry, anything that would set her mind at ease, and she could leave knowing that she had experienced something inexplicable and leave it at that.

On shaking legs, a jolt of pain from her ankle, Kate stood and turned around. Cluttering the attic were piles of boxes, some of them with extinguished candles on their tops. One of them had an old bayonet, rusty and covered in dust, it looked like it belonged to the Second World War. Yet what she had come here for was just before her, not five feet away. This time Kate's heart did not pound, her vision did not go blurry. Instead, she remained where she was, scrutinizing the rotted fabric of the wedding dress, the mummified skin beneath, the bared teeth and empty eye sockets, the tipped over stool by the hanging body's feet. With the morning sunlight to illuminate it, the body was not half so frightening. Unexplainable, irrational, and grotesque to be sure, but not scary, and relief washed over her; she was not going crazy.

But she had to be sure.

Kate took a step closer and reached out her hand. She avoided touching the exposed ribs and the blackened, withered heart that lay still and unmoving within. On top of the body's head, there was a veil raised over its skull, much like her great-aunt Sylvia had worn last night. This, she knew, would be more than enough. But she hesitated just before touching the fabric.

Wasn't seeing this enough? Could she not just leave with the image of the body scarred into her brain?

Her fingers twitched.

No. She needed the second opinion of another sense, so she reached out and grabbed the veil by the loose end near the skull.

Kate felt her body shudder as a pulse throbbed through her hand and up her arm like a jolt of electricity. Screaming, she tried to pull away, but couldn't move. She closed her eyes, and when she opened them again, the body before her had changed, its dried skin becoming thick with flesh, ice-blue eyes that bulged from their sockets. The body kicked and squirmed, her hands clawing at her throat from where the rope crushed her larynx. Her tongue protruded from her mouth, teeth bared and digging into the thick, purple flesh between them.

This was not the worst of it. Not by far, for as Kate tried her best to pull away, she realized that her face was mere inches from her own. Her own face that turned purple, then black, squirming under the weight of death, her eyes that dug holes into her own, that pleaded for help, for release, for peace from this living hell.

Ba doom ba da doom.

The ragged heartbeat echoed in Kate's ear canals, getting slower and slower, fading...fading, until the body ceased its kicks and its arms relaxed and only the final throes of death made the body jerk and spasm. And both of Kate's bodies slumped together, forming one mass, one body. And through the murky darkness of Kate's vision, she saw black hands reach up to her through the shadows. The hands of death, they grasped her with cold fingers that stung, and pulled her down, down, down …

* * *

"I don't know why you're so angry!" Kevin said. "It's only six months. I'll be back before you know it."

Kate turned to face the living room window. Outside and down the street, men in fatigues were marching. They mocked the sinking dread deep within her stomach with their presence alone.

"It's crazy over there," she said, fighting tears. "We see it on the news every day. Car bombs, ambushes, and all the things they don't tell us, but we hear about anyway."

"Nova Scotia, Germany, Afghanistan, it doesn't matter," Kevin said, as though he had not heard her. "You act the same every time I get an assignment where I can't bring you."

He sounded desperate, a little angry himself. But he had no right. No right at all.

"Fuck you, Kevin," she said, surprising herself at how calm her voice sounded. "Go over there and play hero with your friends, and see if I'm here when you get back."

* * *

This time, the tears did come. They rolled down her cheeks in fat rivers, falling onto the floor like raindrops as she thrust the phone against the wall, picked it back up and threw it repeatedly until it finally shattered.

She had lived alone on the base for four months without her husband and they use the telephone to tell her?

The tears blurred her vision as she returned to the living room, the sound of her feet falling with the weight of a giant's. The housing unit belonged to the military, the same people who had sent Kevin to his death. And so she picked up the nearest lamp and threw it at the television, and when that didn't give the satisfaction she desired, she picked up the television and threw it as far as she could. It shattered and popped and then lay still.

When she was done, the bottom floor lay in shards of shattered glass and plastic, with Kate on the floor, panting, and once again fighting the tears.

* * *

As the military housing people turned their cheeks, as her husband's former commanders came by to escort her to the airport, the tears did not return. At home, finally home, nothing looked the same. The pitying looks from her old friends and family members only managed to fill the emptiness with anger. With hate.

They could smell the alcohol on her breath. Kate could tell by the ambiguous way they wrinkled their noses when they reached in for a hug.

Don't be so melodramatic, the eyes of her old friends seemed to say.

The hypocrites. These friends. Most of them were married, with children, their own husbands working normal nine to five jobs.

They didn't understand. They didn't *know*.

Only the eyes of the old seemed to know. They looked on her with a knowing not only of her situation, but of the darkness that now dwelt within her belly. Her mother, for example, who had come to her a month after the funeral, holding within her hand the directions to what she called a cottage.

"You need to get away from all this," she said. "You need time alone. To heal, to come to terms with your new self."

* * *

And somewhere in the darkness, Kate knew she could survive this pain. All she had to do was open her eyes, face the ghosts from the past and present, and go home.

Only, she wanted the closure that had been denied her, the closure she had denied herself. She should not have let Kevin go over to his death with anger tainting their final good-bye. She should have answered the telephone or responded to at least one of his weekly letters. But the road of life was paved with should haves, was it not?

Kate opened her eyes to candlelight, to her great-aunt Sylvia kneeling down beside her. Her eyes and lips were black, her breath a foul mixture of rotting vegetables and ammonia. She smiled and her teeth were unnaturally white and sharp.

"My pets, they come to me after they've died elsewhere," the long dead woman said. "They come here in their new forms to lick wounds that will never heal. You can't escape this. I know through experience. I know through the pain and anger that dwells within me still, after all these years."

Sylvia raised a hand, motioning at the hanging body, no longer resembling Kate, but back in the state which Kate had first seen it, rotted and dusty. Beside the body, there hung a second noose. It was empty. Saved just for her.

"You can join me," Sylvia said. "You can end it all and join me and my pets."

Kate sat up and noted that sunlight no longer shown through the attic window, and from outside, the hounds of the previous night howled and snarled. Aunt Sylvia moved to let Kate stand, and moving over to the second noose, she bent down and readjusted the stool that lay on its side.

"You've already seen what it looks like," Sylvia said, and when she turned to face Kate again, her complexion had returned to the soft, glowing grey with the large, amused eyes Kate had met her in. "You *know* what it must *feel* like."

From within the exposed chest of the corpse, the black and withered heart began to beat its unnatural rhythm— *da boom ... da ba doom*—and again her great-aunt smiled. The smile looked innocent, childlike, in the candlelight.

Outside, Sylvia's pets howled all in one chorus. A requiem sung just for her? Kate looked up at the second noose. It wasn't as though she hadn't already considered it, back when she first learned of Kevin's death, when she had returned home to friends who didn't understand, to older relatives who understood all too well. She would have done it not to be melodramatic, as her friends' eyes might have suggested at her husband's funeral, but to escape the pain, the anger, the regret and guilt.

But she was stronger than that, otherwise she wouldn't have lived long enough to have come here, to this house, to her great-aunt's lonely and insane ghost.

"No," she said. She looked to her left, knowing what to do, how to end this. The bayonet she had noticed earlier still lay there. She turned again to Sylvia as she picked the bayonet up.

Sylvia's scowled as though knowing what Kate was up to, her face once more collapsing into the dark rings that surrounded her eyes, her grey lips going black. She hissed, spittle flying from her mouth.

"You little bitch!" Sylvia screamed. "I'll kill you myself."

Kate didn't give her the chance. She thrust the bayonet into the hanging corpse's chest, through the ribcage and into the withered heart. Hot, black blood spurted onto Kate's hand as the mummified corpse began to kick and thrash, as Sylvia screamed as though the blade had pierced her own heart. Another gust of wind and the room fell to darkness. The wind, much stronger than last night, pulled and pushed at Kate's body all at the same time, forcing her to hug the corpse so that she did not fall. Finally, the corpse began to settle, the wind died off, and Kate stepped back, still holding the bayonet, the blood painting her hands like ink.

Moonlight lit the attic. Aunt Sylvia was gone. Momentarily or forever, Kate had no idea. Heading for the trap door, the corpse faded and then disappeared altogether, as though it had never been there. Both nooses nonexistent.

Kate headed down the steps, down to the second floor. She took her time, not wanting to sprain her other ankle, or stab herself while carrying the bayonet, heavy and real within her grip. This she would take home as proof, a souvenir, a reminder of how close she had come.

* * *

Outside the air was cool on Kate's skin. Shivering, she thrust the bayonet into her belt strap and headed down the front porch and onto the yard. The bodies of the hounds lay spread out along the ground, all the way into the forest. Upon closer inspection, however, Kate realized that they were no longer wolves. They were men, wearing the malted green or brown uniforms from over a hundred years of military history. The uniforms of over a million Canadian soldiers.

One lay right at the tip of her feet. Kate wiped at the tears building in her eyes, then looked deep into Kevin's empty gaze.

"I love you," she said.

She bent down farther and kissed him on his lips. They were cold and lifeless.

When she stood up again, the bodies began to twitch with the sound of breaking sticks and clothing rustling together. Lifeless no more, the men moved, turning, sitting on their haunches, getting up on their feet. In five minutes the dead soldiers were all standing, surrounding her. Their stare was lifeless, but it was Kevin she concentrated on. She wanted to reach out and kiss him again, to hold him in her arms. But before she could move, they were turning away, moving together as one solid unit. Their animated forms were soon silhouetted by the moon.

"Good-bye," Kate whispered.

None of them acknowledged her. Instead, they disappeared, one by one, into the forest where they would never return. It was as if Kate had inadvertently allowed the hounds to show their true forms when she had stabbed her aunt's cold, black heart. But this was a good thing, for they were no longer the woman's prisoners.

They were free.

And so was she, Kate realized. Not better and far from healed, but free nonetheless.

She smiled and wiped at the wetness in her eyes. A chapter in her life had closed with the soldiers' departure, leaving behind a new and mysterious creature wearing Kate's skin, and so she headed to the SUV, got in and turned over the engine. And then she drove away.

Chemical Burn

There was a time when Alex hated his job; five nights a week spent with him on his knees, scrubbing brown specks and crusted yellow stains off a sea of porcelain. Tonight, he wears yellow gloves while he scrubs white tiles and toilet basins below. But the damage is already seeping in through his nostrils, absorbing into his lungs. He knows his mistake now, the mixing of chemicals with human waste, the mixing of chemicals all on its own. It sinks into the blood, and after months of exposure, breathing it in, it changes how flesh works at remaining alive. New ideas are borne, and suddenly, kneeling down to scrub isn't so painful, so humiliating.

You can be a god, the voice whispers, its strained vocals echoing down the large bathroom corridor. *All of you can join as one.*

Somewhere close, the Chemist is laughing.

Closing his eyes, he can see Brandon and Colleen, elbow deep in their own shit and piss. They pause and stare out into the oblivion that is slowly receding to immortality. They close their eyes, and Alex can feel their inner eyes crawling over his skin like ants. As one, their eyelids flutter and open, and the universe is before them, all black skies and white flares of distant starlight: a kingdom of night that is without end to either sorrow or blessed agony.

* * *

Above, starlight glitters. Alex shakes his head, rubs at the spot between his eyes where the pressure is building. The ground before him is a graveyard of cigarette butts, empty junk food wrappers and plastic cups. The cool night air bites at exposed skin, and as he approaches the Pontiac, he adds his own half-smoked cigarette to the litter.

From behind, Colleen and Brandon head to their own cars. They walk slowly from the arena as though they wish not to leave, yet their expressions are content, fulfilled. Something deep within Alex's stomach rumbles, and a violent current suddenly explodes into his esophagus, up into and through his mouth to splatter the pavement below. Alex bends to avoid getting the vomit onto his shoes, but the greenish, foamy liquid splatters upon black leather, black denim, and it smells of black cherry chemical.

"Jesus," Brandon says, approaching Alex from the left. "If I didn't know better, I'd swear you're drinking the shit." His laughter is cruel and unwelcome; the bitter music of it fills the silent morning as he steps into his Chrysler.

"I can feel it squirming inside my veins," Colleen says. Her voice is calm, yet somehow ecstatic. "Like a living breathing entity, joining my blood, my heart, my very thoughts." She smiles, then enters her Dodge. Its engine roars to life, and within seconds, Alex is feeling better, standing alone with a cloud of exhaust permeating above to block out the glittering sky.

Inside the Pontiac, he shivers, starts the engine, turns on the radio, and he is free, driving down Headonville's small downtown district. It's 3:45 in the morning and Dunlop is nearly empty, save for the few junkies, the wandering homeless, and two women dressed in furs and jeans.

The scarves wrapped around their necks look like psyche-delic snakes, and when he pulls the Pontiac over, they ap-proach, seeking warmth and companionship.

"Are termites getting you down? Be instantly gratified! Dial 1-800-yura god, and be bug-free this time tomorrow."

The radio is loud, drowning out the women's voices, and so Alex turns it off, rolls down the passenger and driv-er side windows.

"Hey, Alex. You looking for some fun tonight?" Doris, African American, her skin like chocolate, leans down so that Alex can see her ample breasts, the cleavage leaving little to the imagination. She pokes her head inside, her breath sweet and hot on his cheek while she waits for an answer. On the passenger side, the second also leans in. Her name is Sally. She is smaller, her skin milky-white, breasts like swollen mosquito bites.

"Maybe he wants both of us," Sally says, and then gig-gles.

Alex smiles and leans his head back. He thinks num-bers—dollars and cents—before letting his imagination run wild. But his head is swimming within thick carnal gunk, and he nods, indicating for both women to get in. Money be damned, or as Brandon would put it, "Instant fucking gratification."

* * *

When he gets home, the Chemist barely reacts to the women. He sits at what Alex considers the kitchen table, jugs of cleaning solution surrounding his feet; the test tubes, beakers and a dropper before him on the table are all full of the noxious chemical that glows bright yellow-green, the same color as the Chemist's naked skin. He holds the dropper above his opened mouth, and drops of liquid-narcotic land on his tongue. His entire body shivers violently as violet eyes roll up behind drooping eyelids.

You should put this shit on the streets. Although his voice fills the bachelor apartment, his mouth does not move, and the girls do not react. *We'd make a fortune.*

Ignoring the Chemist, Alex turns on the television, takes off his shirt, and sits down on the bed. Doris and Sally waste no time. They are on him like leeches, their lips sucking and kissing his neck, his chest. They move down, knowing what he likes. He leans back, head resting in cupped hands, and the television glows up there on the ceiling, from where there is a commercial playing, the commentator stating, *"Order now and you too can be a god!"*

Through the din of television and sucking sounds, the Chemist's laughter is unpleasant, mocking, yet easy to ignore. Alex reaches over and grabs a vial of chemical from the nightstand. Uncorking it, he breathes in the vapor. It burns in his lungs, and instantly, the world becomes clearer, the sensations of the women working him all the more extraordinary. His body melds with those of the prostitutes' into one massive, squirming worm of flesh. Pure, God-like pleasure, and Alex's own laughter joins with the Chemist.

* * *

Alex had come across the chemical compound by accident, in the first month of his job at the Andy Anderson Arena cleaning toilets and sweeping floors. Having three bottles on the counter at the same time, their misplaced lids the apparent mistake. Sweeping the floor of the cleaning room and not minding where his elbows went as he moved, Alex turned around and all three bottles fell to their sides.

The chemicals mixed on the counter by the sink, and then a vapor rose into the air like cigarette smoke. Cursing, Alex put the broom aside and began to clean up the mess.

The bottles were of different cleaning products. The largest, Mr. McSpiffy, an all-purpose cleaner; the second was bleach. The third was the acid toilet bowl cleaner, an acid so strong that it often sent similar clouds of vapor into the air as the one Alex worked hard at not breathing in as he cleaned the chemical spill. Soon, however, the vapor was everywhere, impossible to avoid. It burned his sinuses, his throat and lungs, and then, without any supercilious waiting period, the world began to change around him. The lights became brighter, the specks of dirt more pronounced. The very walls oscillated in and out as though breathing. And when he closed his eyes, there it was, the universe in all its beauty, and then the tight-lipped words from the Chemist:

You can be a god.

"Instant fucking gratification!" Brandon had bellowed when shown the effects of the gangrenous mixture, his eyes cocaine-wide, pupils acid black disks, the whites marijuana bloodshot.

Alex smiles at the memory, but it dies as he pulls the Pontiac into the arena's parking lot.

While Brandon is from South Headonville, where drugs are as common as tap water, Colleen is from North Side. Her family a part of the ever-dying middle class, she works at the arena not for survival, as Alex and Brandon do, but to save money for school. She was the last to sniff the noxious vapor, the last to fall into its hypnotic trap.

Today, she waits by the Dodge, her hands twitching, rubbing together like a priest about to give sermon. Alex pulls his Pontiac beside her, and he barely has a chance to get out before she is at the driver's side door.

"About time you got here," she says. "Why don't you let me bring some home, huh?"

Above, the moon is a bright silver dollar; an arctic wind has turned Colleen's cheeks crimson.

Alex smiles. "You were the one who said we were crazy for taking the shit," he says, heading for the arena's entrance. "And now you want to take it home, where your parents can find it and trace it back here, to me?"

Following, Colleen says: "You and Brandon breathe the shit like it's oxygen!" She's getting angry now, her childlike voice raising, her hands gesticulating impatience. "It's not fair, and you know it."

Alex stops, turns around to grab her by her arms. She flinches at first, thinking he might hit her, but relaxes when his expression softens, showing her no such intentions.

"Listen, Colleen. You have a future. You have school next fall. You should be thinking about *that*. Not this shit."

A sound like thunder explodes into the parking lot: the roar from an engine that should have died years ago, loud heavy metal music blasting from the cab inside. Brandon swings his Chrysler mere inches away from Alex's Pontiac. All intrusive cacophony dies, and then Brandon is walking towards them, wearing only blue denim pants and a white T-shirt, his head held high against the cold wind.

He walks past Alex and Colleen without greeting them, as though they do not exist in his world. *Perhaps we don't*, Alex thinks, *but that would change if I had forgotten the chemical, refusing to make any here, where his spying eyes would watch, steal, and make money.*

A quick flick of the wrist and the cigarette Brandon holds is airborne. He enters the building without looking back. Nothing can touch the man, not cold air or the people around him. He is invisible, thinking himself a god, a king, anything other than what he really is.

* * *

"One day, I'm gonna shoot every motherfucker who pisses me off," said Brandon.

Soon after Alex had shown Brandon the mixture, Alex went over to Brandon's own small apartment. This was the first time he had ever visited the man, and that night, in a rage over ghosts, phantoms of the past, he held the six-shooter with a steady hand, pointing it at Alex, at the specters standing beside him.

"Pow, pow, pow!"

Laughing like a small child, Brandon put the gun aside to uncap his vial of chemical, breathing deep its toxic vapor. Alex sighed, his eyes nervously wandering around the room. Surrounding them, on the bed, on the floor, were dirty clothes and pornographic magazines. Standing on Brandon's television and up on shelves, displayed like trophies, were empty bottles of *Canadian Club* whiskey and *Smirnoff* vodka. Scattered ashtrays were overflowing, and the smell of human sweat, of something more pungent than even that, Alex feared would take forever to wash out of his skin and clothes.

"All of them," Brandon said, all laughter gone, his eyebrows knotting. "Dead. Instant fucking gratification."

Brandon picked up the gun, aimed its barrel under his chin. His eyes were wide, his grey teeth reflecting the room's dim light through a tight-lipped smile. Ghostly fingers traced Alex's spine, turning his blood cold. Up until now, Brandon hadn't pulled the trigger. His finger, in fact, had not been anywhere near the trigger. Holding the gun with suicidal fervency, as he was right then, however, the skin of his finger turned white from pressure.

Click

The sound filled the silence, and Alex's bowels turned to water. The gun was empty, and Brandon pulled the trigger a second and third time.

Brandon's laughter followed Alex out of the apartment and into the hall where it bounced off the hallway's thin shell. Alex should have never come here. Most certainly, he would never return.

* * *

When Alex and Colleen enter the Andy Anderson Arena, they are still arguing. Brandon sits in the cleaning room, six vials of chemical that refuse to react any more rest beside him on the table. His presence is a sharp blow to hurting egos and the constant craving for substance, so Alex and Colleen become silent. They look at each other, all arguments on what's fair forgotten within the crease of their eyebrows. A new question has taken form within the thick, oppressive air.

But Brandon answers it for them:

"You know, Colleen brings up a good point," he says to Alex, his voice deep but calm as though holding back what he really wants to say. "How long are you going to keep the mixture a secret? We could be rolling around in money right now. We could have quit this useless job."

The Chemist laughs in Alex's ear, his words from the previous night a whisper through the silent room: *We'd make a fortune.* Colleen's eyes grow wide as she looks around the room, her face growing pale. Brandon, however, barks his own laughter, all the while he stares at Alex with that skin crawling glare.

"Yes, a fortune that should be mine!" he shouts.

"Brandon, what are you talking about? We agreed to

keep the chemical mixture between ourselves, for our own use."

Brandon smiles, shakes his head. Feigned jovial attitude then dies as his fist slams on the table, knocking over the test tubes and spilling their useless contents. Brandon had stolen the test tubes from Fritze's, a bar on Headonville's single downtown strip. He had come in to work the next night looking proud, stating that the glass vials would be perfect to contain and use the substance safely, with each of them using only one or two a night. He was right; the only problem was that over the weeks, his vials had grown in number, while Alex and Colleen both maintained the original arrangement.

"No, *you* agreed to that," Brandon said. "Not me."

Losing patience, Alex places his shoulder bag carefully onto the table. He takes out six corked test tubes and rolls them Brandon's way. "Why don't you take some of that, huh? Might make you feel better."

Brandon does not hesitate. He uncorks the closest vial to him, inhaling deeply, violently, his pinprick pupils suddenly gaping abysses as blood vessels turn the large white's of his eyes red. Watching this, Alex moans inwardly, wanting to experience the same rush, a dreadnaught blowing the delicate fabric of reality into space with its cannons. He resists, the dread in his gut telling him that whatever is up Brandon's ass is far from reaching conclusion. Instead, the drug is feeding the man's quest for power, for street riches. Alex can see it in the smile that spreads across Brandon's lips, his eyes now relaxing but losing none of their intensity.

"Make me feel better?" Brandon says, his complexion paling, spittle splaying on bleached lips. "I feel like a fucking god."

* * *

Nights pass under Brandon's emotional dictatorship. His consumption of vials grows from six to eight, and he does not let up on new ideas of entrepreneurship. Perhaps he sees it as a way out of his one-room apartment and the incessant stench of his own scent. Whatever the case, he is like a child as he wanders down the arena's many hallways, his work untouched, arms upraised like some Christian about to fall into seizure at a revival.

But it's those black eyes that haunt Alex the most. When he's at home and in bed, they dance behind closed eyelids, staring at him accusingly.

Tonight they watch, they follow, they hunt. Around corners and in the shadows, Brandon is always present. His eyes always scanning him, that smile never leaving his face. It's as though he has become something else, something not entirely human.

"*Whack your arthritis pain in the rear-end,*" the speakers from above say. "*Buy today, and become a god.*"

Brandon looks up, then back down to Alex. Those eyes, liquid tar, and Alex wants to look away, but is unable.

"You haven't taken the chemical, Alex," he says. His voice is deeper than normal, almost metallic. When Alex was a child, he had a Transformer toy. Optimus Prime. On its back, a small rubber hose that had turned his ten-year-old voice into something robotic. Although Brandon's voice reminds Alex of this, his voice is fleshier, like some Old Testament demon struggling to sound human.

"You disappoint me," the Brandon-thing says. "You had so much potential."

* * *

The only thing that truly had potential was the drug Alex had accidentally created. Three days without inhaling its noxious fumes, and Alex is in bed, wide awake, sheets chilled with his sweat. He tosses, turns, thinks about Brandon and Colleen. Mostly, he thinks about the chemical mixture, how it burns into lung tissue, forcing its way into the blood stream. He laughs into the silent night, the Chemist and his sardonic comments blessedly absent. Chemical burn would be the perfect name for the drug, if he ever were to put it out there on the street. But as he shivers, his stomach gurgles, and he is up, heading for the only other room in the apartment. In the bathroom, his bowels release liquid frenzy, which would foam up like soap under the nefarious chemical's hallucinogenic influence. Dead sober, it smells and looks biological, as it should, and pain shoots through his abdomen, electric jolts to make him collapse upon himself as he sits there, on the toilet, the laughter having long ago turned to tears.

Time passes. Hours, days, weeks, Alex does not know. He only knows that he had closed his eyes, and now there is a dull knocking, muffled through paper-thin walls, and a persistent, "Alex, hey Alex. You in there, man?"

It's Brandon. Tonight, his voice sounds like it should.

"Hold on," Alex says, his own voice sounding hoarse and weak. He cleans himself up and pulls his track pants back on, his legs cramping and the cheeks of his ass sore.

Exiting the bathroom, Alex heads for the front door. He opens it. Brandon is standing there, his elbow propped up on the doorframe, his skin nearly as grey as his teeth.

"You need to get off the shit," Alex says. "I don't think it's very healthy. I don't see how it can be physically addictive, but I'm sick."

"You got it all wrong, brother," Brandon says, then grabs Alex by the hair at the top of his head, forcing him back into the apartment. He closes the door behind him with the heel of his boot. Only inches away, his black eyes penetrate Alex, digging into his own like knives.

With his free hand, Brandon pulls out a test tube, full of vapor. All in one motion he pushes Alex onto the bed, pinning him there, uncorks the vial, and covers Alex's mouth. "You need to take your medicine," he says, and Alex has no choice but to acquiesce. The vapor snakes its way up into his nostrils, into his lungs, where it burns.

"That's right, breath it all in. Happy Friday!"

The world around Alex changes. Light becomes brighter, colors more vivid. Brandon smells of vodka, of body odor and unwashed laundry, his breath a deadly mixture of rotting gums and bacteria. Again his voice is the demonic Optimus Prime drawl of the night before.

"It's time we have ourselves a night on the town," he says, letting go of Alex once certain that the drug is taking effect. He then heads for the kitchen table and picks up vials, all full of chemical. Stuffing them into the pockets of his winter coat, he looks down at the ingredients and laughs.

"Bleach, Mr. McSpiffy, and toilet bowl cleaner. I should have figured."

Alex stands, his heart pounding in his chest. The pain in his limbs and guts, his head and eyes has dissipated, but he notices that Brandon's skin has turned to tar, to match the inky blots of his eyes. It is like a black hole standing before him, sucking in life and light, and he wants Brandon to go somewhere else, to leave him alone. But he is holding the same six shooter he had on that one night Alex had visited his dwelling. He points it at Alex's chest. The smile on the man's face is the vicious snarl of an ape's, ready to pounce and attack, and Alex does not doubt that this time the gun is indeed loaded.

* * *

Outside, the wind whips at Alex unrelentingly. He shivers, crosses his naked arms, wishing he had brought a coat. Brandon follows close behind, the barrel of his gun sticking painfully into his back. They cross the street, to where the rusty, dented pick-up waits. All the while Brandon speaks, whispering madness into his ear.

"The time for confusion has reached its end," he says, that demon robot voice churning Alex's stomach. "Know that distorted fragments of reality can shift, they can play games. It takes strength to overcome this, to bend the fabric, to bend space and time to your will. To *my* will.

"Instant. Fucking. Gratification! And tonight, we will introduce this power to the world. But first, you must find the control for yourself."

The Chemist stands beside the truck. He is smiling, wearing that all knowing, I told you so, look on his face. *We could be kings*, his eyes seem to say. *Kings with no throne but the money we make, the car we drive, the clothes we wear, the music we listen to. It's all here, Alex, all within the chemical burn.*

Brandon shoves Alex into the driver's seat, tossing him the keys and telling him to drive. As Alex fastens his seatbelt, Brandon slides into the passenger seat and turns on the stereo. Old commercial jingles blare through the ancient speakers, crackling with electricity. A storm is on the way, and Alex wants to laugh at the thought, laugh at the warped world before him, the various artificial, drug-induced colors and the way the street before him twists and turns—Brandon's precious fabric of reality, of space and time, taking its own shape within the ether.

He does not laugh, though. Brandon's gun is sticking

into Alex's ribs. It hurts, and his laughter would only bring the ride to a violent stop. Which could happen anyway, as the truck veers ominously into the opposite lane after pulling out onto the street.

"Clear the shit from your mind," Brandon hisses. "Force the clarity to take shape, and drive as if you are sober."

"You're fucking crazy!" Alex says. "You'll get us both killed."

"I'm *not* crazy!" For a moment, the gun moves away from Alex's ribs. Brandon rubs his face with his free hand, and then the gun is back, poking even harder. "You need to experience the control, and then *use it*. It's a matter of survival."

Like you'd know anything about survival, Alex thinks, but keeps it to himself. The way he lives, it's a wonder he's survived this long at all. Although the chaos of Brandon's life mimicked his own, what with the bachelors apartment, the substance abuse, Alex does not want to die. Not like Brandon does. Death, or some version of it, already exists inside him. It peeked into the world through his blank, dead eyes, through a smile never truly felt. Now, death stares at Alex, tight-lipped and scowling, its precious pride wounded.

To live with such demons, Alex could not imagine. He does not feel sympathy, or even fear, but he does change his hypothesis. Brandon is perhaps a survivor after all.

Perhaps.

"Drive faster!" Brandon yells, and Alex does as told. Not because he is afraid, but because he sees Brandon for whom and what he is: a body without a soul, an empty shell working on instinct alone. And because of this, Alex can see through the psychedelic haze, the colors and distorted vision. It's like pressing buttons at some mental control board. All he has to do is hit the right ones, and the universe is at his disposal.

You're better at this than I had thought, the voice of the Chemist says. Although Alex suspects that he is speaking to him alone, Brandon's eyes grow wide and the gun is again absent from his sore ribs. As with the other night, Brandon has also heard the Chemist's typically silent drawl. He turns off the stereo, looking around frantically within the truck's cab, his pupils dilated to thick, black disks. He opens his mouth as though to say something, but the Chemist is quicker, his voice drowning out all other sounds within the truck's interior.

If you were to close your eyes, you'd see all the stars of the universe. If you were to look closer, you'd see just how big it is, and how insignificant you are in comparison. You would have learned that you could not highjack what is not yours and inflict your will upon others without eventual consequences. You would have learned that death is absolute in its oblivion, just as is your heart, thoughts, and existence.

The latter frightens you the most, as it should, as it will continue to do so, should you choose to continue down this path, learning nothing but what the ramblings of your mind tell you. You must learn that you know nothing and never will.

"It's the voice of God!" Brandon screams, his voice breaking, rivers of tears flowing down his cheeks. Still, he is holding the gun, listlessly in one hand, pointing it at the truck's ceiling. Taking no chances, Alex hits the gas. Trees and telephone poles blur by them until Alex is certain he can handle the outcome.

He cranks the wheel to the right, hoping to aim the truck in just the right spot. Traveling off the road a few meters, the truck slams into something steady, a tree unmoved by the truck's violent velocity. Glass cracks and shatters, the shards mixing into crimson blood that looks like crude oil in the moonlight. Metal crunches, and every- thing is suddenly motionless and silent, save for the ring- ing in Alex's ears.

Pain that is like fire spreads through Alex's torso and pelvis, but he is certain that nothing is broken. The blood, in fact, comes mostly from Brandon, soaking the dash- board before them. He lays crumpled on the other end of the truck's cab, and once the ringing in Alex's ears sub- sides a little, he can hear the man weeping.

"The very voice of God has spoken to me," he says to Alex. "He told me that I am nothing."

As we all are.

Time passes in silence, with both men staring at one another, the existential horror in Brandon's eyes enough to make Alex laugh, and this time he does.

"What's so fucking funny?" Brandon asks, and Alex laughs even harder.

"You're so naïve," Alex says, pointing to the stereo and the jingles that no longer play. "You believe everything you hear."

Alex then reaches for the door handle, unclips the seat- belt, and is then standing out in the cold, his legs shaky and body hurting. Brandon says nothing, makes no move- ment towards the gun that lays on the floor by his feet as Alex turns and heads back into town. It'll be a long walk without at least a sweater, he knows. But the night sky above is a canopy of shining stars free of clouds. No voices follow him home. No auditory hallucinations to keep him company. Alex doesn't mind, content as he is with the scent of late winter and the brilliant glow from above.

The beauty of it is almost mystical, mysterious in its spirituality, and Alex smiles.

* * *

Alex pulls the Pontiac into the Andy Anderson Arena parking lot. He is not surprised to see Colleen there, waiting for him under the glow of the streetlamps, her hands fidgeting. She wants to experience the divine again, the test tube direct link to God and all His wisdom. He is also not surprised that Brandon has yet to arrive. All weekend, and no word from the man; not on the six o'clock news saying that he'd been found dead on the side of the road, or a phone calls from the boss stating that he had quit.

Still, Alex's gut tells him that Brandon will not return. The chapter is closed.

He parks beside Colleen's old Dodge, and before he can get out of the car, she is there, looking at him with a smile on her face.

"'Bout time you got here," she says, but leaves it at that.

Together, they walk into the arena. She does not mention the drug. Instead, she says, "I saw Brandon yesterday. His face looked about as good as yours does. Did you two get into a fight?"

"You could say that," Alex replies. "What did he tell you?"

Colleen sits, resting her arms on the cleaning room table. "Not much. Says he's going away and plans on not returning. Said something about family he's got, living down south somewhere. He told me to tell you that he's sorry about Friday night, whatever that means. But I don't believe he's really going away for good."

"I think he had a profound experience that scared the shit out of him on Friday," Alex says. "So I wouldn't give up on that notion."

"Oh really?" Colleen says, her back straightening, eyes hunger-wide for something juicy. "Care to tell me about it?"

"Not today," Alex says. "Maybe some other time."

Colleen feigns a pout, her wormy bottom lip protruding, eyes downcast. Alex doesn't budge, and so the pout fades into something real, and she once more begins to rub her hands together in that nervous, fidgeting way he had seen when pulling up the Pontiac to park beside her.

"There's something else I wanted to talk to you about," she says. "It's about the drug."

Alex raises an eyebrow.

"It's just that … last week you told me that I had a future. I thought about it all weekend. And I think you're right. When I saw Brandon, it sort of drove your point home."

She sighs, as though frustrated at her inability to open up and tell him what's really on her mind. Her hands, meanwhile, lay relaxed, on the table.

When she speaks again, her voice is louder, more confident. "I just don't want to end up like some junky, strung out all the time, before I even get the chance to do what I really want."

Silence then. Always the silence. And then, "Are you angry?"

Alex smiles and closes his eyes.

This is what he had wanted for himself, Colleen, and perhaps even Brandon. Behind his eyelids, the stars of the infinite and utterly mysterious universe glitter and shine with a million pin pricks. The universe right there, as it always was, waiting for them to take charge and find their way through the labyrinth. And although Alex thinks he can hear the sardonic laughter of the Chemist, the very voice of God, it is distant, far away.

"No," he finally says. "I'm not angry."

And with that, and a final nod of understanding, they head off to work.

Room 118

Nothing spectacular hit me about the room. The door, in fact, looked like any other entryway inside the building: rectangular frame, pukish green paint, a doorknob. I mean, what was so goddamned special about this one room? Why did everyone step to the other side of the corridor when passing it?

Yet they, my new co-workers, looked at *me* as though *I* were insane. I never once hesitated walking by room 118, never looked at the faded-green door as though it might decide to move by itself, jump and attack.

I remember my first night working the gymnasium. Brenda, the one training me in the art (art, as she called it) of cleaning toilets and sinks, made only a brief remark about the formidable 118 while we were passing through the labyrinth of corridors, from bathroom to bathroom.

"Room one-eighteen," she said. "Stay away from that room, and don't ever let me catch you trying to get in there. The room is evil. Loves nothing better than to consume stupid little pinheads like you."

Okay, not so brief, but I did not give much thought to what she said. Perhaps Mr. Greenwood, the gym's proprietor, held secret documents inside or something. Maybe he'd hogtie and shoot my sorry ass if I ever tried to get in.

Later that night, while Brenda was vacuuming the carpets in the front lobby, I made the mistake of pausing at room 118. Okay, not pausing, exactly, but putting my mop-bucket aside and stepping up close—my hand reaching for the bulbous doorknob, and ...

... was that the sound of a heart beating from inside?

My hand touched the surface of the doorknob. It felt warm and inviting. The pulsing beat from inside beckoned my entrance.

"Just what in Sam's *Hell* do you think you're doing?"

I jumped, and turned to see Ed. He stood at the corridor's end, his face red and purple and his eyes as big and bright as light bulbs.

"Uh, just dusting the doorframe," said I, now certain of room 118's off limits status.

"We don't touch that door," Ed barked. "We *never* touch that door. And more importantly, we never go *in* that door. You understand, boy? Or am I gonna have to drill it into your skull?"

* * *

I am an educated man, got a B. A. in literature, so Ed did not have to tell me more than once. Never once did I touch or try to enter that door for the next few months. I kept my distance, ignored the call of the beating heart.

It is unfair of me to say that I was the only one not intimidated, as there was another. She never once bothered to shift sides of the corridor when passing the room. Her eyes were sharp. Looking longingly at 118's frame, the expression on her face told me that she wanted to go in there and confront the superstitious demon pounding in her chest. Her name was Natasha, and we became quick friends.

"Why on earth would you want to work here if you're

so goddamned smart?" Natasha asked me on that first night.

"Apparently writing a novel and getting it published is a lot more difficult than I had assumed."

"Well, duh!"

'Duh!' How often I wished the ability to look at life in simple terms as the rudimentary syllable 'Duh.' 'Duh' does not even make a real word, and this is perhaps the reason why I wanted suddenly to add precious Natasha to my life.

* * *

"You want to take me to the movies and dinner?" Natasha said, and laughed. "You're a fucking bookworm, look at the way you dress just to come to work! You look like a freak cleaning toilets with that tie, you know that?"

Natasha did not acquiesce to my advances right away. Given time, she would crack I knew. I just had to find the right words to smooth the edges, to dig myself in—so to speak.

"And you're obsessed with room one- eighteen," she went on, "like you want to go in there, or something. I mean, come on—get a grip!"

"Ah, but I see you staring at that room every night!" I said. "I think you're projecting yourself."

"What the fuck are you talking about?"

"Dr. Carl Gustav Jung? The Swedish psychologist and his theory of projecting the things you don't like about your-self into the characteristics of others?"

Natasha's cold, blank stare gave me the shivers; warn-ing me not to pursue the subject.

* * *

I grew up in this small town of Pine River, then moved to Toronto for four years to attend university. Looking back, I wonder, what was I thinking? Why did I not major in a subject holding the potential of going somewhere, like accounting, law, or medicine?

Yet, I have loved reading and writing since childhood. I have penned poetry and short stories while reading volumes of books covering many genres throughout my history. A bookworm I am indeed, though I was not without friends.

Richard and Mike were there the day I left for university. They threw me a *Dungeons & Dragons* going away party. Like loyal comrades in the trench warfare of high school unpopularity, Richard and Mike were there the day I returned.

"Why didn't you write to us, man?" Mike asked while rolling dice during my first visit back. He was attempting to build a new character, for a game in the midst of creation.

"Yeah, asshole," Richard added. "You could have at least phoned!"

I held back. How does one explain the complicated subject of escape? Because escaping Pine River and its dead-end future was precisely what I was trying to do. Moreover, how does one explain that companionship is more interesting in the city? Where I received invitations to *real* parties, where girls actually *liked* my reading habits, and intellectuals read poetry in smoky cafés?

"You never call anymore," Richard complained a month or so later. I was trying to get ready for work. "It's like we don't exist in your world."

Since I began working at night, I've become something of a hermit. The midnight shift has a way of sucking life away from its victim. At first, you think working at night is great, you have the day in its entirety ahead. Yet soon it sinks its carnivorous teeth into your skin, injecting poison, exhausting not only your body but also your thoughts. You think: I'll sleep today, hang out with Richard and Mike tomorrow, but tomorrow never comes. Because every day is tomorrow. You come home when the sun rises having worked through your body's natural sleeping time. No matter how much you sleep, you can never get enough. You are tired all the time, grow sensitive to bright light— like the sun—and become irate over simple problems.

"You look wiped out, man," Mike said. "And pale. You should, like, go to the doctor or something."

"Yeah," agreed Richard. "And what the fuck is all this talk of room one- eighteen?"

* * *

The sound of a heart beating called me, as though I were the only one it wanted. While others swayed over to the other side of the corridor to avoid it, I hung close to the right. I hugged the wall, wanting to touch the doorknob's tingling warmth once more. I rarely did, considering how the others usually reacted. So I suffered the scorn of courage.

"You're fuckin' insane, you know that?" Ed often barked.

"Why do you do that?" Irene whispered. "You make me nervous getting so close, like."

"Remember what I told you," Brenda scorned. "I ever catch you trying to get in there, you'll have my foot up your ass!"

Natasha, however, never once looked at 118 with foreboding wisdom. Indeed, she eyed the room with an expression akin to passion.

When I broached the subject, Natasha bulked. She claimed no such curiosity, or admiration, of room 118.

"What's so goddamn important about that room, anyway?" I asked. I am certain that she had once asked Brenda, Ed, or Irene the same. Her sigh gave this away.

We were sitting in The Pine River Coffee Shop—told you she'd come around—after watching a ridiculous movie about a vampire slayer.

Natasha tilted her head in thought. "I have no idea," she finally admitted.

"Come on, are you saying that you never once thought about it? What's inside?"

"Of course I think about it. But shit, what does it really matter?" She sipped from her coffee. "They probably keep it locked if it's so fucking important, anyway."

"*You*?" I said, flabbergasted. "Are you telling me that you, the non-conformist, wearing black everything all the way to your lipstick, don't want to know what's inside? Simply because it's off limits?"

Natasha's cheeks turned red. I was surprised. I had never before seen her blush.

She cocked a thin, black eyebrow, and despite the redness of her otherwise pale cheeks, she shouted, "Fuck you!" catching the attention of the many other consumers. "You're such a shit-fuck! Why don't you go in there if you're so fucking interested?"

Her finger pointed threateningly at my face and her cheeks grew redder with each progressive syllable. When she was done, she grabbed her purse and stormed out of the coffee shop as if I had insulted her.

Across the dining area, old ladies shook their heads at me, disapproving of my behavior. The old men sitting beside them looked upon my sorry state with sympathy. That was in mid-July, on a Friday night. I wonder what I would have done had I known that this would be the last time I'd see Natasha. Perhaps I would have hugged her, kissed her, anything but let her go.

* * *

Natasha Pearson's disappearance caught the media's attention throughout Ontario. The police, on a widespread hunt, stated to various media outlets that this was the fourth missing person in ten years for Pine River. And with all of them unsolved, the cops were not about to let this one go unanswered.

The police questioned me, of course, because I was the last one seen with Natasha. Witnesses had reported our 'having harsh words' that night in the coffee shop—the old bags and their pathetic husbands.

I later learned I was not the only one scrutinized under the law's suspicious eye. The cops questioned Ed and Brenda once finished with me, then moved on to Irene. On our first night back to work, Irene told me in her quiet, whispering voice that the police had inquired about Brenda and Ed during her interrogation. They had worked the longest at the gym, ten years from when the Pine River Fitness and Aquatics Center first opened. Ed and Brenda had also worked with all three of the other missing persons, Irene having worked with only one.

"His name was Andy," Irene whispered in the darkened corridors, amongst the mop pails and supply carts. We stood close to the formidable 118, close enough for Irene to shoot an occasional nervous glance its way.

"You remind me of him, Nick," she continued, "always wanting to know about *that* room, like. Except Andy was worse. He always touched the doorknob; always put his ear to the door's surface, like."

Here, Irene paused. She placed her hands flat together in prayer formation, and rested her head upon them. Her face was smooth with pleasure to demonstrate Andy's relief at being near room 118.

"He did this for months before he went... Well, he was here, working, the night he went missing. He stole the master key off our cart. We found it in one-eighteen's keyhole. Just like Natasha."

I blinked several times. "Natasha came here, to that room, before disappearing?"

Irene's expression turned from sorrow to disappointment. "Get with it," she said, her whispery voice louder than I've ever heard it, "Natasha came and never *left*."

"Why didn't the police go in there and find her, then?" I shot back.

"Because they did! When Mr. Greenwood was here, during the day!" Irene's frustration at my inability to comprehend the situation made her tremble, ceasing the nervous glances to 118. "They found nothing but what *is* in there. An electrical room."

* * *

Ah ... Mr. Greenwood, the Pine River Fitness and Aquatics Center's proprietor. The name stuck on the back of my tongue like bitter tasting glue for weeks. I tried phoning the bastard during the day, here at the gymnasium. I even drove over to the gym to pose my questions, yet he was never in.

I also tried him at his home—getting his phone number and address was not a problem considering I clean his office—but he never answered the phone. When I drove over, I met a large house surrounded by inactivity: no car in the driveway, the grass in much need of a cutting, and no answer to my fist excessively pounding on the front door.

How the police contacted Mr. Greenwood, I'll never know.

* * *

Natasha.

Her last words haunted me to the point of permanent insomnia …

'Why don't you go in there if you're so fucking interested?'

In my own way, I had—now that I think about it. After two weeks of investigation, leading nowhere, the itch of no sleep crawled inside my head like spiders spinning webs across a drained mind.

I tried finding consolation in my old friends, Richard and Mike. First, I went to the liquor store and bought a twenty-six ounce bottle of whiskey. I then traveled the short distance to knock on their apartment.

"If you're going through some trouble," Mike had told me at the front door, "then why can't we just, you know, acknowledge it without actually having to talk about it?"

Apparently, they had found girlfriends through some Internet dating system. They had dates that night, in fact, or so they told me.

Later, alone in my own bachelor apartment, I sat on the floor listening to the mournful music of *Radiohead*, drinking the whiskey straight from the bottle.

I thought about contacting newer friends from university, but found myself instead on the phone with my mother.

"Are you drunk?" she asked.

"No. I mean yes."

"And I suppose you're with those two dunderheads."

"Yes. I mean no."

"You need to take better care of yourself," Mom said. "You don't want to end up like your dead alcoholic father, do you? Hey, are you going to be okay? I know you miss your friends. Don't cry like that! I don't want to have to hospitalize you."

Through all my years of unpopularity in high school, I never knew the true meaning of despondency. I should have never called my mother, but she was the only one.

* * *

The night shift plodded onward, slow and mundane. For days, we had to work shorthanded—which was no easy task, considering the size of the building and all the summer sports clubs that frequented the place—until the gym's staff found a replacement. Our checks kept coming in, all signed by Mr. Greenwood's accountant. Yet the man himself remained a mystery.

Our replacement was some kid by the name of David. He had graduated from high school in the spring, and wanted to save some extra money for university.

Brenda trained David, and I couldn't help but chuckle at the speech she gave him. The same one she gave me when I first started. "Room one-eighteen," she said, "stay away from that room, and don't ever let me catch you trying to get in there," etcetera, etcetera.

Later, David questioned me about it. We were outside, David enjoying a cigarette, and I the fresh night air.

"What's up with that room," he said, "room one- nineteen?"

"Eighteen," I corrected.

"Yeah, whatever. That guy, Ed, nearly tore my head off just before we came out."

"What were you doing?"

"The fucking prick! I just touched the door, to see if it was locked. And he was right there, man, threatening to kick my ass. *I'd* kick *his* ass if he wasn't so old!"

"And what were you doing *touching* the door?" I yelled, ignoring David's need to kick the ass of anyone yelling at him. "You know it's off limits, so why bother?"

David tossed his half-smoked cigarette into the bush. "What's with you people?" he said and stormed back inside.

* * *

The steady throb of the beating heart in room 118 grew louder, more intense. Yet, I seemed to be the only one who could hear it.

Ed, Brenda and Irene had their hands full during this period watching both David and I. They kept their eyes more on me, as though they were worried.

I had since lost the title of the "insane" one. This rite passed to David. Poor David, how amusing it was watching him get flustered and angry with the subject of room 118. The young chap reminded me of myself, yet a new curiosity straddled itself upon my psyche—David's infuriating obsession of room 118. My heart froze and my blood turned to ice whenever he looked at it too longingly, or tried to touch it.

When David talked of room 118, I wanted to see him bleed from the thrashing of my fists. Yet I held back; I had no energy to pick fights. Fighting had never been a part of my construction anyway, so the thought remained fantasy.

During lunch breaks, I marveled at Ed's threatening

glares shot David's way, even when David sat eating quietly. Brenda's expression often resembled a scornful mother while Irene's nervous disposition never faltered.

"How do you do it?" I asked Ed one fateful night. "I see the way you look at David. How do you restrain yourself?"

"I'm too old," he said. "Besides, I never kicked the shit out of you, did I?"

I nodded my agreement.

"Anyway, it goes with the old adage," he went on, "the night shift sucks the life outta ya, like a magnet to a battery. I've been doing this for years now, kid. If I were you I'd find someplace else to work before it sucks you in, too."

Again, I nodded. Having watched Ed in the kitchen during lunch lift a shaky spoon to his sunken, thin lips for months astonished me. Or, the way Brenda often stared into space, sometimes coming out of the trance giggling. Irene often rocked back and forth in her chair, as though awaiting the apocalypse. If working at night was so hard on them, then why did they come in night after night?

I had learned of Brenda and Ed's previous careers once we stood on better terms. Brenda was once a nurse, Ed a roofer. Both did not work at night for the money, as Brenda's husband was a doctor, and Ed had made enough money while standing on people's roofs to retire for the rest of his life.

What drove them in every night was simple need—they *wanted* to work, to keep themselves busy.

Irene, however, was a widow who did need the money. Natasha had once told me that Irene began working midnights three years ago, only days after her husband's funeral. My heart bled for her in that kitchen with each nervous glance, in every whispered word. Natasha had also told me that Irene was not always so fragile. Before her husband of twenty years died, Irene was a housewife and an active member of her church. She had a strong voice that traveled far whenever duty called. The church children paid attention to her during Sunday school class. Natasha knew this because she had once been one of them.

"So, are you going to clean toilets for the rest of your life?" Ed barked, snapping me back.

"No," I said. "But I like it here. The pay's not that bad, and nobody messes with you."

Ed frowned, cocked a suspicious eyebrow.

"Okay, you're right," I said, "I don't want to do this. I want to write. But fiction is not a profession one can apply for. It takes a lot of time."

Ed nodded.

"You got any plans this weekend?" he asked.

"Not that I'm aware of."

* * *

The summer was nearing its end. Saturday night was cool and crisp, allowing my breath to turn to mist before my eyes. I stood by my rusted Pontiac, enjoying the fresh air. I felt mesmerized by the full moon and its illumination of the entire sky, even though I could not stop yawning and stretching sore, aching limbs.

In the few days since my talk with Ed, David had left us for university. No love lost there. Mr. Greenwood's staff replaced David with yet another high school graduate who lived with his mother.

"Are ya kiddin?" Phil, the new kid, had said during Brenda and Ed's questioning. He had told us that he planned on living with his mother forever, he never wanted to get married or have children, and held no ambition to pursue further education or even find a better career.

"I've got it made at home," he had said. "Mother don't give a shit what I do, and she don't ask for too much money."

The strange thing about Phil was his reaction to Brenda's "Don't go near room one- eighteen" speech. She took him along that stretch of corridor, even pointed it out to him, but he only shrugged, and said, "So?"

"Boy won't make it on this shift," Ed had told me out of Phil's earshot. "He don't even care about an important room like that!"

The blinding glare of headlights turned into the parking lot. An old Ford pickup, the cabin crammed with three bodies, pulled up beside the rusted Pontiac.

"Glad to see you could make it," Ed barked, crawling out of the truck.

"Wasn't sure if you had the balls," Brenda said, and laughed.

Irene gave me a nervous nod and whispered a silent "Hi."

The four of us stood in a line, looking at the Pine River Fitness and Aquatics center.

"If you want to skimp out," Ed remarked before we headed inside, "now's the time to do it. Ain't nobody here think any different of ya for it."

* * *

Inside, a tall, dark man stood by the entrance of our destination. His presence there reminded me of a phantom Dracula. Long, pale fingers held a flashlight pointed at the wall beside him. The light exposed his pallid face and receding hairline of jet-black hair. When he smiled at our approach, his teeth seemed large, and sharp.

The heart beating inside room 118 throbbed, pulling me

to its threshold from where it pounded, steady and rhythmic. I could feel its gushy pulse inside my head, drowning spiders.

"So this is our boy?" the man said.

"This is him," Ed responded, beaming, his hairy eyebrows cocked high upon his forehead. He sounded nervous, yet there was also fatherly pride in his voice.

"Glad to hear it. I suppose you know who I am," the man said to me. "You've been trying to get in touch with me for quite some time."

Although he did not look like any owner of a gym, I nodded. "Mr. Greenwood."

"Now that we know each other," Mr. Greenwood said, "shall we proceed?"

Brenda, Irene, and Ed pulled out small bottles from their pockets. Mr. Greenwood did the same and they surrounded me in a tight circle.

"Not everyone who passes through this door comes out the other side," Mr. Greenwood said. "Are you sure you wish to proceed?"

I looked over to Irene, who turned guiltily away. At the time, I blamed her for lying to me. Had she told me the truth about Andy and her involvement earlier, I might have been able to find Natasha.

"Yes," I said.

Mr. Greenwood uncorked his bottle, poured a black substance into his hand and smeared it on my forehead. It felt like jelly, cold, wet and sticky.

"This is the rite of initiation," Mr. Greenwood said. "With the blood of the successful, I hereby summon you, Nicolas, to take this challenge with courage and stealth."

My fellow night-shift comrades did the same, their bottles holding either the blood of the triumphant, or the blood from past failures.

The circle then formed into an anxious knot behind me, and Mr. Greenwood unlocked the door to 118. From its inside, I heard the call of better things, a better life. Dreams and hopes of false futures stared at me in the face. They beckoning my entrance, begging my advance to a battle I would surely lose. With it came sporadic voices— inarticulate whisperings—and a great light that warmed cold, shivering skin.

My heart, beating its fury, found the rhythm of the pulse from inside. With one hesitant step, the warm light immersed my cautious self.

I then heard the door close behind me. When I turned around, the light grew faint, collecting itself into a vertical rectangle just to the right of the door—a black mirror, reflecting a shadowy human form.

I watched this human form mutate for hours it seemed, until I was staring at myself. This dark reflection resembled a beast, a demonic version of everything that I am.

This was not what I was looking for. I grabbed the door-knob, but it was locked. My heart pounded painfully in my chest, and as my demonic-self reached its hands out, passing through the black mirror's border and grasping the edges, I forgot everything that ever mattered to me. Including Natasha.

The demon stepped through from whatever reality it had existed, and stood inches from my panic-frozen body. Then it reached out, cold and slick fingers wrapping around my head, puncturing my eyes, and filling my nostrils and mouth with what tasted and smelled like copper. Blind and mute, I tried to scream but nothing came out. Then my demonic-self spoke the word, "Sleep," and my body obeyed ...

* * *

… And I awoke upon cold pavement, staring up at the endless, starry night sky, the constellations alien and utterly new. I stood to find that the shadowy bulk to my left was not a cliff as I had imagined, but the front to a large house. An ancient mansion, it seemed, right out of a black and white horror film with its door slightly ajar, opening and closing in the night's frosty breeze. "Natasha?" I called into the darkness within, but no answer came forth. Instead, there was the sound of snapping twigs and the grunt and growl of something big from behind.

I turned around to face nothing but blackness, and as my eyes began to clear, a large and billowing forest rose upon the hillside in the soft moonlight. Two glowing orbs at eye level, pacing, going left to right, left to right just inside the tree line, and my heart sank and once more began to pound. When the creature pounced, its large, feline body charging my way, I let out a yelp and ran into the house …

* * *

… And I stepped inside the front foyer to the Pine River Gym. My head swam with vertigo and broken reality, and I turned around to find relief at no horrendous beast having followed me. Through the disorder, however, came the sound of a beating heart. It throbbed through the empty corridors as though the building itself was alive, with me standing inside its ribcage. I took a step forward, wondering what I was to do next, when, from around the corner materialized the form of Natasha. She stood looking much as she had when I had last seen her, black eyeliner and lipstick, black skirt and blouse. She motioned for me to approach, but when I did, she disappeared.

Thinking I knew the answer to this game, I ran down the corridor, took the first left, and found room 118's threshold. The beating heart was strongest here. I reached out and touched the door's surface, the rhythm pounding slightly against the palm of my hand. I closed my eyes, spoke the name "Natasha," then reached down and grabbed the doorknob that liquefied upon my touch and swallowed my hand, my arm, my body until its gushy pulse and throbbing gel surrounded me and ...

* * *

... And I opened my eyes to a room with familiar objects and fluorescent lighting. To my front was a row of treadmills, elliptical and rowing machines. Surrounding me, attached to the walls visible in my peripheral, were three rows of chairs with what looked like people sitting on them. I did not look at them, I felt as though I was going to vomit, and when I sat down on the closest treadmill, I noticed the televisions. All of them hung over the chairs, one television for each, and all of them were on. The television within my direct sight showed a child of twelve or thirteen, primitive in culture, painted in black, white and red, using the edge of a razor sharp rock to reach between his legs. One of his tiny hands held the foreskin to his penis, the other wiggled back and forth with the rock in the task of self-circumcision, his face expressionless but focused.

All the televisions, nine in all, showed either flashing words or something terrifying, something real. Lions jumped on a zebra's back, their claws dragging the animal down, their teeth at the animal's throat and tearing into the skin in a spray of blood. Soldiers fought hand-to-hand combat on some unknown battlefield, bullets and bayonets tearing skin and chipping bone. The encasements to the televisions were of a human skin color, and fluctuated as though breathing. Behind them, large, thick black tubes ran down before the crimson walls, down into the people inhabiting the chairs. The tubes ran through their cheeks, up their nostrils, down their throats, and the inhabitant's eyes rolled up into their skulls as though being fed some noxious drug.

At first I didn't recognize any of the inhabitants, until I focused on the girl sitting right before me. Black hair, black eyeliner and clothes, Natasha trembled in her chair, the cables that dug into her flesh and facial orifices feeding her images of pain and wonder.

This was more than I could take. I screamed, then turned around, looked for an exit, but there was none to be found. No windows, no doors. I spun around in circles screaming, desperate for the nightmare to end, when a voice cut through and silenced me.

Take your seat. The voice was low and calm. *Watch the undertow unfold.*

The chair beside Natasha was empty. Above, the television flashed the word *Undertow*, its cables snaking down and reaching out to me. My breathing slowed, my heart calmed, and for a moment, I wanted to sit down on the chair, let the television show me its visions of violent nature and the rite of passage. I could sleep in its embrace forever in the endless supply of external dreams and fantasy. In this room, I could die.

Perhaps Natasha had saved my life. Perhaps it was my own naïve loyalty, but I did not want to bow down to this fate simply because saving her was more important.

The snake-like cables reaching out to me were inches from my face. Somehow, in my daze, I had managed to approach a few yards, any closer and I'd have been their willing victim. Instead, I reached out, grabbed them, two thin, one thick, in both hands, and pulled. The room came alive in my defiance, the fluorescents flashed, the images on all the televisions skipped with static and snow, and the inhabitants, including Natasha, began to kick their legs, their arms swinging in epileptic spasms. I pulled until the cables tore free from their home, and a black liquid sprayed onto the walls from the behind the television.

Wasting no time, I dropped the torn cables and ran over to Natasha. She jolted at my touch, and as I grabbed the cable jammed into her throat, her eyes unrolled from behind her skull. Alert and focused, she looked at me, and once the cable was free, she shook her head, reached up and clutched my arm.

"No," she said. "I want to be here. If you don't, then go away."

Her hand, clutching my arm, found the cable I still held, the one that was down her throat, and in my shock, I let her take it. I stepped back as she raised the cable to her open mouth and let it squirm its way back down her esophagus. Once the cable had stopped, the room once again settled down. The televisions showed horrid visions, and their inhabitants began to relax. For a long moment, I stared at Natasha, at all the others, and suddenly I didn't want to be in this room any longer.

When I turned around, I wasn't surprised to see my evil double, the thing that stepped out of the mirror when Mr. Greenwood first closed the door to room 118. It smiled at me with sharp teeth. It tilted its head and raised its fist. And when it punched me between the eyes, I saw stars, and then darkness.

* * *

I woke the next morning upon the cold interior of 118's floor to the loud humming of electricity. Blood clogged my nostrils and stained my T-shirt. The blood had gathered into small puddles around my head. I sat up and tried to remember what had happened, but was lost.

Well, not completely lost.

Mr. Greenwood sat at a card table. His dark eyes narrowed after I sat up, focusing on me.

"You should be proud," he said. "Not many get the chance to partake this rite of humanity. They do not have a room of one-eighteen's magnitude. And not all the ones who do survive."

"What is this room?" I asked, my mouth parched and tongue lolling. For a long moment, I didn't think he would answer.

He pursed his lips and tilted his head—an almost elegant gesture. "You can think of this room as a gateway," he finally said, "to many wonderful worlds your mind cannot comprehend."

Mr. Greenwood stood up and approached me.

"Congratulations," he said, offering his hand. I took it and he thrust me onto my feet.

"You'd better go home and get some sleep. Take tonight off, with pay. My treat."

I turned to leave, but paused at the door. The sound of glass scraping on the concrete floor gave me the shivers. When I turned back around Mr. Greenwood knelt by one of the fresher puddles of blood, scooping it into a tiny glass jar.

He looked up and smiled.

"Have a good day," he said.

"Who are you?" I asked. "Where do you come from?"

His smile died, and he looked away, daydream-like, as though remembering things best left forgotten. Then a small smile spread across those thin lips, and he looked back at me, and said, "I come from somewhere very far away from here, Nicolas. A place more frightening and beautiful than what you saw last night can ever be. I built this building ten years ago, and with it, this room. I built it not for people to get into physical shape, as any gym would dictate, but for special people, like yourself, to exercise their minds, their souls."

Despite the possible good Mr. Greenwood and his surreal electrical room had done for me, I looked down at him as he scraped my blood and felt a knot of loathing tighten inside my chest. I left the room wanting to see *him* on the floor, *his* shirt covered in blood.

* * *

I cannot say, for certain, if the things I saw while inside room 118 were ever real. All I can tell you is that the experience, although dreamlike in content, was nothing like a dream at all. From the time I woke up upon the porch of some ancient house to when I found Natasha strung up by a breathing television, everything felt as real as it does when walking down the street, driving a car, or cleaning a toilet. It was as though my unconscious mind had taken control of the conscious in a great hallucinatory adventure. Yet, to call it hallucinatory is wrong, because I was there, and suffered the wounds to prove it.

I took that Sunday night off, as suggested by Mr. Greenwood, and the next night at work, Brenda, Ed, and Irene were all waiting for me to offer excited slaps upon my back. They told me that they had always known I'd make it. Although I smiled at their kindness, I felt excluded from their joviality. I had failed in my attempt to save Natasha, and yet another part of me was satisfied leaving her where she was. If inside that room was where she wanted to be, then who was I to object?

Fortunately, this feeling of failure did not last. And although I was different inside, and I do not know if the change was for the better, I do know that I respected life more. The span of time we get to live upon this planet is relatively nonexistent. We are merely visitors with one main choice: to either live or die. And I chose to live.

After my adventure in room 118, I never saw or talked to either Richard or Mike ever again. I also never saw Mr. Greenwood, as he had returned to the cave of his hiding. In the months following, I found myself an accomplice to the games of the nightlife at the Pine River Fitness and Aquatics Center. I shuffled over to the other side of the hallway whenever passing the formidable 118, and I heckled those who caressed its vomit green door with their eyes. I continued to ignore the call of the beating heart, and a few months later, during the winter, I parted ways with the gymnasium altogether. Although my co-workers were sad to see me go, they understood that it was time for me to move on.

A part of that place, however, still exists inside me. No matter where I am, or what I am doing, I often pause, the sudden onrush of thought and memory flooding my mind so completely that I can almost smell Natasha's perfume, hear Brenda's and Ed's warnings or Irene's nervous whisper. And for one moment, I am back within the gym's corridors where I stand somewhere near the rhythm of a beating heart, wondering what is so damn special about room 118.

Surviving the Fittest

Charlie Paulson could picture how he and his sister would die. Everyone they had ever known, after all, had died. All of them violently. So, maybe it was reasonable that in their own case, and perhaps because of their deceased friends and family, Charlie saw various versions of their deaths every day: masses of undead surrounding him and his sister like a moving, animated wall, their teeth tearing out of rotted gums as they tore flesh from bone. With none of the living around for hundreds of miles, their screams going unanswered. He thought these thoughts so often that he began to wonder if he'd developed some form of new obsession, the dark fantasies a ghost that followed him wherever he went so that he couldn't even enjoy a peaceful moment with his sister, as they had before the rising.

Right now, however, death was not a fantasy borne of constant fear. It was imminent. Inevitable. The only difference was that Charlie had not imagined it happening this way. With Chuck Holten, though, he should have seen it coming.

The tip of Chuck's double barrel shotgun pointed at Cindy's head. Crying, she held her hand up close to her ear, her fingers doing a panicked dance in the air as she cringed, clenching her eyes closed tight.

"Why can't you shut her the fuck up?"

Charlie gaped like a fish. "She doesn't understand what you're doing," he said. "Take the gun out of her face and maybe she'll stop."

"I'll take the gun outta her face when she's either shut up or dead!" he yelled, yet he didn't pull the trigger. Instead, he did as Charlie had suggested and placed the pump action on his shoulder. He paced, a feral dog deciding which of its prey to dig his teeth into first.

"Why did you invite them to follow us if you're just gonna kill them?" Sylvia said. She sat on the bumper of the old, beat up Chevy, her skinny ass barely making an impression on the dirt encrusted chrome. She nodded her head at Charlie and Cindy who were on their knees. Her salt and pepper hair fell over a face that seemed too young for greying hair. It barely managed to cover the bruise that took up the entire right side of her face. All the other members of Chuck's group stood in a tight circle around them, many of them urging Chuck to just pull the trigger already. Others stood with their arms crossed, their faces unreadable.

"Because I thought they'd be useful," he said. "Instead, we got ourselves a chickenshit and a retard!"

Charlie and Cindy had come across Chuck and his band two days ago while walking the roads. They had just lost their friends, Dale and Merrick, who had been helping Charlie with Cindy, helping them both survive for six months since the uprising. Cindy was still upset, her hands in constant motion, her eyes always wet. Her moans and sudden outbursts never seemed to stop. Charlie figured that not only was she mourning the loss of her friends, but that she knew somewhere deep inside their survival was now reliant on her brother's abilities alone. Dale had been a large man, with thick muscles roped around his forearms and legs and a deep inner wisdom for survival. Merrick, his wife, was also physically fit, a force of nature all her own. Charlie often switched with Merrick in taking care of Cindy while the other two went out for supplies. Dale always said it was best to teach Charlie how to look for supplies in case the unthinkable were to happen.

The unthinkable did happen, *must* have happened. Close to two weeks ago, Dale and Merrick had left for supplies but had failed to return. Charlie waited for over a week, had exhausted what was left of their food waiting.

Wait no longer than a few days, Dale had always said. *Hell, after one day, if we're not back, then we're dead. It'll then be time for you to find food of your own, like I taught you.*

They wandered the country streets looking for food, looking to stay alive and no longer weary of the undead that lurked in the surrounding forests and fields. Perhaps it was naivety on his part, or maybe it was just how young he was, but Charlie never thought that the living could be dangerous, until they met Chuck.

"You knew she was retarded when you picked them up," Sylvia said. "So, what changes things now?"

They were about to make camp for the night in a clearing of the woods just off the road, near an old garage, when a small army of the undead interrupted their temporary peace of mind. Charlie had helped assemble the first tent when the first gunshots were fired, after which he had lain on the ground, his hands covering his head. Cindy had sat on the ground beside him, screaming and pulling at her own hair.

Surrounding their circle, the recently walking dead lay in heaps on the ground amongst skull fragments, rotted brain matter. There was also the body of a man unknown to Charlie, one of Chuck's right hands. His throat had been torn out, and he lay not far from where Charlie and Cindy sat, staring up at the sky with grey skin and a surprised look on his face. It wouldn't be long before the man would sit up and try to bite the first person it saw.

"Yeah," Chuck said to Sylvia, his eyebrows raised, eyes wide. "But I only took them in because *you* said it'd be a good idea. I don't *have* to keep them."

Somebody in the small crowd laughed and said, "Damn right!"

Sylvia ignored this, barked laughter of her own. "Well, if that's the case, if *you* don't want to take care of them, why not just let them go? You don't have to shoot them."

"Maybe I wanna shoot them," Chuck said, and he returned to Cindy, pointing the double-barrel at her face. Cindy, who had grown quiet without the gun pointed at her, restarted a fresh wail that was ear-piercing, but Charlie did not dare to react. Not with Chuck in a homicidal rage, and although Sylvia was arguing on their behalf, she didn't seem all that serious in her intentions. She remained leaning against the Chevy Truck's bumper, smoking a cigarette.

"That's enough," a new voice said. It was Bob Taggard, a man whom Charlie had only heard speak when he had introduced himself. Unlike Chuck, who wore jeans and a T-shirt that might have once been white, Bob wore leather pants and a leather vest over a denim shirt. Out of all of them, Bob looked the fiercest, the meanest, his long hair and bushy beard, the snake tattoos wrapped around his arms doing nothing to help Charlie think otherwise. The man stepped into the middle of the circle and grabbed Chuck's shotgun by the pump action, his muscles bulging in the fading sunlight.

"They're just kids," he told Chuck, his mouth a straight line.

Chuck met the other man's eyes. "What're you gonna do about it, huh?"

Both men's attention shifted suddenly. Breaking the silence was the sound of sticks snapping in the woods, of feet dragging upon the earthen floor, and what was worse: the well-known and much feared moan of the undead.

It sounded as though they had surrounded the band while Chuck contemplated murder.

Both men continued to stare at one another, only now the color had drained from their cheeks.

"Lovely spot to pick, Chuck," Sylvia said. She was off the truck's bumper now, a gun in her hand, the cigarette bobbing in her lips as she spoke. "Real fucking safe!"

Chuck ignored her and jerked the shotgun out from Bob's slackening grip.

"Only the fittest survive this hell," Chuck said to Charlie. "You'd be wise to remember that."

"For God's sake," Bob said. "The kid is what, fifteen?"

"Gotta learn sometime," Chuck responded. He then turned to his men, now standing in ragged lines, all of them facing the evening shadows ready to fire their weapons. The undead had obviously heard the first gun battle, which was short, and all the yelling that had happened after that.

The first shot was fired, the loud sound of it bouncing off trees and bodies.

The screams came next, frantic and high-pitched so that Charlie could barely tell they came from men. All around the brother and sister was commotion, with both the living and the undead. Gunshots from shotguns and rifles and pistols put holes into rotted flesh, turned flesh into chunks of airborne debris. But it wasn't enough. They kept coming. Chuck wanted Charlie to prove to him that he was brave, that he wouldn't lose it during a battle. But the man hadn't even armed him. How was he supposed to fight in this?

He grabbed Cindy by the arm and pulled her onto her feet, which wasn't difficult; she was already clinging to his ribcage. Her mouth sputtered incoherent words, words that sounded like, "Momma," and "Dadda," and he was surprised, perhaps even a little hurt, that she still thought of those who had died when things got sticky.

He headed in the direction of the old garage he had seen earlier, which looked as though it was probably abandoned long before the first corpse had taken its first step. The sun had set and the darkness was complete. Was, in fact, like a wall of ink. His heart pounded, the hair on his arms raised, but he pushed himself to take the next step.

And then the next.

Out here, away from the main battle, he had only his free hand to act as his eyes, his nose radar-like for the walking dead. He could smell them, but their pungent stench wasn't so strong here, and so he pressed on, going as fast as he felt was safe.

Cindy continued to cry, but he no longer had to drag her by her arm. She clung to his chest in a bear hug, making it hard to breath. In the week since their friends had disappeared, he'd grown used to this form of suffocation; was once annoyed with it, but embraced it now. Could not have taken that next step without it.

The stench got stronger, so suddenly that Charlie barely had time to react. His outstretched hand slammed into something cold and moist and moving of its own volition, and the typical moan of the undead, sounding too much like a siren, drowned out the screams and gunshots from behind.

Zombies moved slowly. They were easy to run by and

avoid if there weren't too many of them. The only problem was their strength. If one got a hold of you, you were finished. Game over. Charlie had never been this close to a zombie before. His instinct was to push it away, but cold, dead and bony hands wrapped around his wrist in a grasp so painful, he feared that the bones would snap and grind to dust.

As it pulled greedily at him, pulling him no doubt to its gaping maw, Cindy began to squirm in his other arm. She cried out, which only excited the zombie further, but Charlie refused to let her go. If he did, Cindy would be out there alone. With all these undead, and with Chuck running around, she would never survive.

Something brushed passed his right side, a quick motion that resulted in an audible crunch at Charlie's front. The zombie loosened its grip, but did not let go. The motion happened a second time. There was a second crunch, and this time the zombie let go.

"Come on." The voice was rough, a whiskey voice, his father would have said. "The only safe place around here is up ahead."

Cindy again relaxed, her arms returning their vice-grip around his ribs.

A hand grabbed Charlie's right arm and dragged him forward, and they were jogging through the darkness, tree branches scrapping at his face, coming close to poking out an eye. Thankfully, it wasn't long before they came to a clearing, the rear of the garage facing them, derelict and falling apart. Gunshots continued from behind. Some of the screaming had faded, but it appeared that no one was following them.

Even though they faced a door and a window, the man holding Charlie by the arm pulled him around to the front of the garage, where its main entrance hung off its hinges.

They entered the building, where blinding light and a long hiss made Charlie squint and cover his eyes. Cindy cried out, and the whiskey voice said, "Sorry. Next time I'll warn you."

When Charlie eyes adjusted, he was looking up into Bob Taggard's bearded face. He held a flare in one hand, a rifle in the other, a knapsack strapped to his shoulders which he took off and dropped to the floor. He looked down at Charlie and Cindy while he did so, his eyes surprisingly soft, projecting only concern. Although he looked like a drug dealing biker—another opinion from Charlie's dead father—he reminded Charlie of Dale, who had taken care of him and Cindy. It was something in the man's spirit, a kindness, a caring for human life other than his own that was absent in Chuck and most of his band.

"We should be safe in here," Bob said. "But I want you guys to lie down on the floor over there in the corner. The dead are everywhere here, and soon there will be some fresh ones to add to that list."

Bob looked at the door they had come through. Charlie knew that he was really looking at Chuck's ill-chosen camp they had escaped from. He wanted to ask if anyone had been bitten or taken down, but decided against it. Bob had shown them only kindness, but he wasn't certain yet as to the man's true loyalties. Maybe he had a friend or two back there. Maybe Chuck was one of them. Charlie doubted it. In the day since getting scooped up by Chuck's travelling band, he had never once seen Bob and Chuck speak together.

"I'm not gonna hurt you," Bob said, as though Charlie was that easy to see through. "But I really need you to go to that corner now. This flare will only attract them. I'm gonna have to do some shooting soon."

Charlie did as he was told. He moved to the other side

of the garage, nearly falling into a pit in the middle, but skirted it at the very last moment. Cindy let out a yelp at the yawning abyss, but Charlie tightened his grip around her shoulder, hoping to comfort her. It didn't work. Bob held out his hand at them, making a *shhh* sound, a silent request to try and keep Cindy as quiet as possible. The man obviously didn't know anything about Cindy or how severe her condition was, Charlie thought. Cindy was like a thirteen-year-old infant, and the only real way to keep her completely quiet when she was frightened or upset was to either sedate her or knock her out. The former of those two options was unavailable; the latter was something Charlie refused to do.

He put a hand around her mouth, talking low and soothingly to her, which sometimes worked. He thought of Dale and Merrick, how patient they were with Cindy, even when things got sticky, and his eyes watered at their loss.

Why did they have to disappear?

Why?

Surely to God they didn't abandon us, did they?

The thought was unsettling, and Charlie would have forced it from his mind, but didn't have to. Sudden gunfire yanked him away from the dark thoughts with the gentleness of a punch in the face. Cindy began crying again, a long and loud wail that nearly went over the sound of Bob's guns going off. She pulled at her hair with one hand, the other's fingers dancing beside an ear. She rocked back and forth, back and forth, despite the grip of his arms.

Bob was yelling and shooting at the odd rotted face that appeared in the window, which was becoming more and more frequent. One of the undead tried to get in through the busted front door. Its stomach was an empty cavern with ribs poking through the torso's midsection. Its face had parts of skull sticking through its chin and cheeks and forehead, all of which had flaps of rotted skin that flaked off as it struggled to fight its way in. It reached, moaning frantically, baring brown and black teeth.

It must have been one of the first ones to turn, Charlie realized. The undead rotted slowly, probably much more slowly than any natural corpse might. This one's body was so rotted and fragile that it actually exploded into pieces when Bob turned his attention away from the window and, noticing it, headed over to fire the shotgun at its chest. Pieces of rotted meat splattered the wall and floor inside the garage, with chunks hanging off Bob's face and chest.

If the gore bothered him, he didn't show it. There were more of them coming through the window and door, and Bob fired, reloaded and fired again. When he had run out of ammunition for the shotgun, he switched to the pistol. Charlie wanted to help him, but Cindy's grip was like steel around his ribs.

The flare Bob had lit fizzed and burned out, throwing the room into a darkness so complete that Charlie thought he could reach out and touch it. Another spark and Bob tossed another flare beside the old dead one, close to his knap sack. Charlie began to wonder if the man only carried ammunition and flares with him. He didn't doubt that he probably did, because Bob had the shotgun again, and was taking care of the undead intruders.

Further gunshots came from outside. Shouting followed and Charlie could see bodies of the undead being taken down from the right. And then, "Don't shoot, it's us." Chuck plowed through the front entrance, which had long ago lost its door. Behind him came Sylvia, a short bearded man Charlie knew as Caruso, and a final man whom Charlie didn't know the name of, but recognized for the large wart on his cheek that stood out like a second nose. All of them had gore on their clothes, their skin and hair. Some of it looked like fresh blood.

"They're almost gone," Chuck said, smiling up at Bob. It seemed to Charlie that everyone had to look up at Bob.

"How do you know?" Bob said.

"Because I know, damn it!" Chuck said. "Don't you question me, or I'll fill you full of lead."

"You can't kill Bob, Chuck," Sylvia said. "He's too useful."

Chuck shot Sylvia a look carved from stone. "Did I ask for your opinion?"

Sylvia crossed her arms and shot a look back at Chuck. Her eyes were bloodshot and wet. Charlie thought that maybe she'd been crying. Perhaps she had lost a friend out there? Whatever the case, her eyes were now digging holes into Chuck's skull, but Chuck barely noticed. He turned back to face Bob, who was looking out the window.

"Yeah, that's right," Chuck continued. "Do you see any of them, huh? Me and my *friends* were taking care of them while you were hiding in here." The smile had returned to Chuck's face, but it wasn't a friendly smile. It looked like a wild animal baring its teeth.

Cindy, who was rocking in Charlie's arms, cried out suddenly, and everyone in the garage, Charlie included, jumped. Chuck looked their way. His lips tightened, his eyes nearly popping out of their sockets. Charlie could see a vein throbbing in the man's temple.

"Now I see what you were doing," Chuck said. "Instead helping out your pals, you were in here, protecting the chickenshit and the retard. What were you planning, huh? Hoping that your old friend Chuck would kick the bucket so you could have the retard to yourself? Good people died tonight, asshole! Some of them were my closest friends.

They could still be alive right now had you been out there, instead of diddling your new treasure."

"You were never my friend," Bob said, his eyes two black holes, a play of light from the flare, Charlie knew, but it still unsettled him. Did Chuck have a point? Did Bob want his sister for ... for *that*?

"Just plug the fucker, Chuck, and get it over with," Caruso, the bearded man, said. The one with the massive wart on his face nodded his head, said, "Yeah, fucking kill him! Then do the others."

Charlie felt his blood turn to ice; it didn't take a rocket scientist to know that wart face meant him and Cindy.

"How did you survive this long?" Bob said. "You do nothing but destroy everything that's in your path. I never should have joined you. You're insane and you're stupid, and you need to be put down like a rabid dog."

The room grew silent, save for the moaning of the dead outside, far away yet still audible. Bob and Chuck squared off for the second time this night, both fingering their guns.

This time it didn't take long for either man to take action.

Both men made the motion at the same time. Maybe it was Bob's size that slowed him down, or maybe he didn't want to win this fight, Charlie would never know, but Chuck's gun was out faster than Bob's. Bullets tore through Bob's torso and neck, and he fell down in a heap without even getting a shot off, his shotgun lying uselessly at his side.

Cindy cried out, her rocking motions becoming violent. Chuck looked up at the garage's ceiling, wiping off splatters of Bob's blood from his face. He looked drunk, Charlie thought, intoxicated with the kill. And when his eyes focused on him, the cold hard concrete of the world below him disappeared. Nobody said a word. Wart face and Caruso giggled like school girls at the violence that Chuck had wrought. Sylvia, her skin pale, eyes glazed, looked as though she were going to throw up.

There was murder in Chuck's eyes. A life of murder, and he wasn't about to stop with Bob. Certainly hadn't started with Bob, either. It was possible, Charlie realized, that Chuck had only picked him and his sister up to kill them.

On the ground now, Bob made choking sounds, his breath labored, his legs kicking, blood squirting from his neck. Within seconds, the man would be dead, and within minutes after that, he would rise again. Yet, nobody was shooting him through the head to prevent it, and Charlie wasn't about to let them in on it if they couldn't figure it out for themselves. *Fuck them*, he thought. *They can suffer with Bob's zombie after I'm dead.*

Like prophesy, Bob Taggard stopped breathing, his legs stopped kicking. Charlie, however, kept his eyes locked with Chuck's. He prayed that the other man read the hatred in his eyes, the silent curses he wished upon this evil man.

Chuck took a step forward. A small grin played at his lips, and to Charlie he said, "I should kill that noisy little bitch first, so you can watch her die. But I think me and my pals here should have some fun with her first. Whaddya say, guys?"

They whooped and hollered; wart face scratched at his crotch.

"Let me have first dibs on her, Chuck," he said. "It's been a long time since I got first dibs."

"You are disgusting," Sylvia said. There were tears in her eyes, a look of repulsion. Charlie wondered how long she had been with Chuck, and if the choice was entirely her own.

"Come on, boys," Chuck said, ignoring Sylvia. "Stevie has called first dibs. I'll hold the retard down, and you," he pointed to Caruso, "hold the boy so he doesn't try and interfere."

Cindy cried out as Chuck approached, almost as though she knew what was about to happen. She jerked in Charlie's arms, and Charlie let her go so that she could run. But Chuck was too quick.

He grabbed Cindy by the arm and punched her in the face, which only made her howl louder until Chuck hit her again, and she fell by his feet, complacent and silent, her eyes open and staring at her brother.

"Cindy," Charlie said, tears streaming down his own cheeks. But he didn't have to take this. Not from them. Dale and Merrick hadn't just sheltered them from the world after their parents had died. If anything, they had done their best to prepare Charlie for people like this. "If something ever happens to us," Dale used to always say, "don't let anyone hurt you. There are bad people out there, Charlie, and they're going to want to hurt both you and Cindy. You'll have to do things that nobody your age should ever consider. You'll have to do some very ugly things."

At the time, Charlie didn't know what Dale was talking about, but it made complete sense now. Steve was at Cindy, waiting for Chuck to force her onto her back. Behind Charlie, Caruso was approaching, a sick, twisted smile splitting the hairs of his beard.

Charlie looked over at Bob's unmoving corpse, at the shotgun lying there, no more than ten feet away. Sylvia was standing there and she was looking at Charlie. For one fearful moment, he feared that she would prevent him from doing what he had planned. Instead, she nodded her head, bent over, picked up the gore covered weapon, and tossed it at Charlie's waiting hands.

Two things happened at once when Charlie caught the shotgun. First, a small group of the undead stumbled through the garage's front entrance. Sylvia screamed, fumbling for her own weapon, which she had hidden in the belt of her pants.

Second, Caruso reached Charlie. He smelled of body odor and bad breath at this range, and the man reached out with his hands, trying to pin Charlie to him and retrieve the shotgun at the same time. Charlie squirmed in the man's grip, thrusting the butt of the gun back so that it slammed between Caruso's legs. The hairy grin Charlie had seen turned into an astonished O, and the man gripped at his testicles and fell back.

Charlie had never felt this kind of rage before. The shotgun shook from his trembling hands; his heart pounded fury through his veins. There was a growl in his ragged breath that he fought to control.

Caruso showed his teeth at him in both agony and rage. "I'm gonna fuck you up for that, little man," he said, but Charlie had no plans to let that happen.

He pumped the shotgun and felt satisfaction at the surprise and fear in Caruso's expression.

"Maybe you've got some balls after all, hey?" Caruso said, and Charlie was about to answer him by pulling the trigger when black and grey rotted hands curled around the man's arms like thick, hairless spider legs. More hands joined in, crawling through his hair and pulling his head back to reveal, standing behind Caruso, a face missing its eyes and nose. Its teeth were somehow white still, and they sunk into Caruso's neck, tearing away skin and muscle, blood spraying in time with Caruso's panicked heart beat. His screams soon became a gurgled cough.

Sylvia stood with a six shooter drawn, but making no move to help her fallen comrade. She looked at Charlie, and he knew somehow that she was enjoying this, watching this man go down. When she turned to face him, though, she didn't need to open her mouth to warn Charlie of anything. Her widened eyes spoke volumes.

Remembering Chuck and wart face, Charlie spun around, but was too late. The first thing he saw was Chuck grab the shotgun from his hands. The second were the man's knuckles as they smashed into his skull, right between the eyes.

The world grew fuzzy with misery, stars shooting through the blurred vision. His knees then gave out and he was falling to the pavement below, the blurriness closing in, bringing darkness and silence.

* * *

"You can't die, you can't die and leave me here alone to take care of Cindy. She needs someone strong, someone who can protect and feed her."

He hadn't realized that he was crying until Dale's large, yet soft finger swiped away a tear rolling down his cheek. They were standing, facing each other in the living room of the house they had lived in for close to six months. His typical easy smile was gone. A grim frown in its place.

"But I am dead," he said. "And you have no other choice. Your sister cannot take care of herself. You're strong enough for that job now. You just need to prove it to yourself."

Dale always looked like a biker to Charlie, but right now he resembled nothing of the sort. His brown hair was still long and pulled back in a ponytail, he still had a bushy goatee, but there was something different about him. A certain light in the man's eyes that spoke of wisdom, of purity. Whatever it was, it didn't last long, for Dale's skin turned blue, the bruised colors of purple and black. His body shrunk into itself, his cheekbones and chin sticking through skin. He was coming at Charlie, his mouth opened wide and displaying sharp teeth and a yawning, ever hungry throat.

Charlie jumped back, and was in a different place. The smell of motor oil and rotted flesh and burnt gunpowder permeated in his nostrils, the mixture making him want to vomit. Or, perhaps it was his pounding head that made him want to be sick. It didn't matter, he could hear his sister crying out, repeating the word that to her represented his name.

"Arlie, arlie, *arlie*!"

The past died in a screen of shooting stars that, at first, covered his entire field of vision, but then slowly began to scatter and go away and he was looking at two men tearing off his sister's pants, laughing as though one of their own had not just died. On the other side, close to the entrance, close to Bob Taggard and Caruso, Sylvia lay slumped against the wall, blood coming out of her nose.

The shotgun was also propped against the wall, close to Chuck, who now held Cindy by the throat, her arm twisted behind her back while wart face fumbled to get his own pants down. They had managed to get Cindy's pants and panties off, and she lay back against Chuck unmoving, her eyes locked on Charlie's. She kicked once lazily at wart face, and then,

"Arlie, elp eee!"

A single tear ran down her cheek.

For a long moment, Charlie didn't move. He was capable of only watching this madness unfold, the fear like a paralyzing drug.

I gotta save her, he thought. *I gotta* save *her*!

But if he moved, Chuck would see it, and he'd be dead. There was nothing he could do but watch and feel his heart breaking.

Just as wart face had his pants down, his hand stroking at his erect penis, Cindy kicked out and up, this time not so lazily. Her foot caught the man right between the legs. Wart face's smile died, became a grimace of pain.

"You fucking bitch!" he groaned, gripping himself and falling to his knees. At the same time, there was movement from behind Charlie, startling him out of his petrifaction. Not only had more zombies found the entryway, but Bob and Caruso began to stir, struggling to get up to their feet. Sylvia moaned, but remained unconscious.

There was only one thing for Charlie to do.

He sprang to his feet, the speed of his movements like lightning, like a superhero, and was at the shotgun before Chuck or wart face could make a move. He put the butt of the weapon against his shoulder, as Dale had taught him to do with a similar gun, and pulled the trigger. Nothing happened. He pulled the trigger again, but the tiny flap of metal refused to budge. He could not move it. Was it jammed? Was it the safety? Was it simply his inability to kill another man, living or dead?

Gunfire exploded within the garage, and zombies coming from the entrance fell unmoving to the concrete floor. Others were behind them, all with various types of wounds and stages of decay.

Chuck fired again, and more fell. Caruso went down with them. Chuck fired until his pistol ran dry, and then he turned to Charlie, a large sarcastic smile on his face.

"That's how you do it, Charlie m'boy!" he was laughing now, a loud, high-pitched laugh. *The man's gone insane,*

Charlie thought, a drop of ice water trickling down his spine.

Wart face had recovered himself. He stood with his pants wrapped around his ankles, his penis flapping around from the bottom of his T-shirt like a dead, shriveled worm. He had a pistol of his own, and he aimed it at the undead without firing until Chuck turned his attention to him, and said, "Well, you gonna just point that thing, or are ya gonna kill some zombies?"

"Fuckin' right!" Wart face said, and the barrel of his gun exploded once, twice, over and over again. Cindy had since crawled close to Charlie, was now holding her head, pulling at her hair.

The inside of the garage was filling with the sharp stench of gun smoke, making Charlie want to gag. But he forced himself not to. He looked at the gun in his hands, at the safety switch on its side. Was relieved to find that when Chuck had confiscated the weapon from him , he had indeed switched the safety on and that the gun wasn't therefore jammed. Charlie flipped it off, and aimed the gun at wart face, the one who had called first dibs on his sister.

There are bad people out there, Charlie, and they're going to want to hurt both you and Cindy, Dale's voice rang through his head. *You'll have to do some very ugly things.*

He hesitated for only a second longer, unsure of killing another man, even if it was to protect Cindy.

But the trigger clicked back, the gun bucked against his shoulder, and it all happened so much easier than Charlie suspected. Pellets tore through wart face's body, chipping skin and bone off his shoulders and arms, burrowing a large hole in the center of his chest. He fell in a heap, remained there, unmoving.

Blood had sprayed Chuck, and he stopped firing, looked

at wart face and then at Charlie as though what he had done was completely irrational and unwarranted.

"What the fuck was that for?" Chuck said, his eyes wide.

Charlie didn't answer the man. He was about to turn and shoot Chuck right in the face, but there was movement from behind him, worm like hands reaching around his shoulders, clumping into fists within his hair. Just like they had with Caruso. The undead had found another way in, and they were swarming around Chuck, their teeth digging into his neck, his skull, his arms and shoulders.

Yet, Chuck did not scream, despite the skin of his face that vibrated, all muscles twitching frantically through the pain. He looked as though he had expected this to happen at some point, and Charlie suddenly understood the man. Understood his madness.

"Pull the trigger," he said. "Kill me."

Although Charlie felt as though he understood a small part of Chuck's madness, it wasn't enough. The man was, after all, about to rape his sister. He didn't deserve the sympathy Charlie could offer with the shotgun in his hands.

Chuck's screams finally came when he saw Charlie lower the shotgun. The undead pulled him to the concrete floor then, their hands digging into his stomach and throat. Wormy bluish-red intestines suddenly appeared in the zombies hands, and when Chuck's screams stopped, there was only the sound of their dry mouthed chewing.

Remembering the undead behind, Charlie turned around. There were less of them now, and Charlie hoped that enough of them had been killed off so that he and Cindy could live one more day. But he doubted it. He thought about pointing the gun at Cindy's head, perhaps from behind so she wouldn't know it was coming. He could do himself after she was gone, and then all this madness would be finally over.

Instead, he knelt down and embraced Cindy. His own tears came when she said his name, hugging him back with her vice-like grip. There was comfort in knowing that she trusted him and only him.

More gunshots erupted. Sylvia had woken up and now stood with a pile of zombies and chunks of rotted brain matter around her feet. She had taken care of whatever Chuck never had the chance to finish off, and she stood there, studying the carnage inside the garage, then ran over to where Charlie lay with his sister.

She brought Cindy her pants, tried to help Charlie put them back on. At first she fought against Sylvia, but when she realized that she was working with her brother, helping her to get dressed and wasn't about to hurt her, she cooperated. Her fingers danced, one set by her ear, the other by her chin. Drool formed on her chin. She held her head at a tilt, and it looked as though she were smiling; the horrors of recent past already forgotten.

Both Charlie and Sylvia envied her.

* * *

"It's a good thing you killed that psychopath," Sylvia said a day later. They were walking through some woods that ran parallel to the road, and she didn't have to say Chuck's name for him to understand who she meant. The sun was setting, but up ahead and across the road, there was a field and an old farmhouse that looked abandoned. It also looked like a great place to squat a few days. Maybe, if the property was free and not infested with zombies, they could stay there for years. Grow a garden during the summer months, one big enough to keep them all fed throughout the year.

But Charlie wasn't feeling that optimistic. He could picture the undead finding them, eventually. He could picture their rotted hands destroying whatever barrier they would build to keep them out; he could picture their rotted teeth breaking as they dug into his and his sister's flesh.

Charlie shook his head. Negative thinking, Dale used to say, gets you nowhere.

But everyone he had ever known, except for his sister, had died.

It was only a matter of time.

"I didn't really kill him," Charlie said. "The undead did."

Sylvia laughed. She was a much kinder person than he had first suspected, now that he had gotten to know her a bit better. As he had suspected, she hadn't traveled with Chuck by choice. He had found her a few towns back, fighting off a pack of zombies with only a baseball bat. After bailing her out, he had told her she could travel with them, that she'd be protected. She soon found that without her baseball bat, she had no one to protect her from him.

"Oh, you killed him all right. Don't let *that* bother you," she said, then quickly added, "he was such a sick, selfish bastard, I don't know how he survived for so long."

The sound of Charlie's laughter was sarcastic even to his own ears. Seemed to him that maybe it took only the sick and selfish bastards of the world to survive this new, chaotic world. He realized then that his new obsession with his and his sister's inevitable and grizzly deaths was not an obsession after all. It was a means of survival, of always being aware of your surroundings. It was the one thing that Chuck was missing, maybe even Dale as well.

Sylvia looked at him, her brow creased, but she remained silent. They stepped out of the forest, headed for the old farm house, the constant moaning of the undead echoing in Charlie's ears. Even if all the zombies in the world dropped right now to never move again, those moans would haunt him for the rest of his life. He looked at his sister, the only thing keeping him alive. Her fingers danced by her ear, but she was smiling and laughing, speaking nonsensical words.

As long as she was happy, he would continue to fight. But for now, he hoped that the farmhouse was empty. He wanted to lie down somewhere comfortable and fall into a long, dreamless sleep.

The Serpent's Son

The movement inside Wendy Clarkson's lower stomach is like a snake uncoiling itself deep inside her womb. She rubs the spot while studying her transparent image in the window across the room. This ghost reflection stares back; her complexion is pale, her eyes as hollow as her cheekbones. Her stomach is large and swollen. The snake fetus moves again, and Wendy's thin, ghostly lips frown.

To Wendy's right are rows of empty forest-green chairs, white walls, and the nurse's desk. To the left, another window with a view of the parking lot from where a woman is quickly approaching. She opens the clinic's door and enters the small glass-encased lobby, giving Wendy's reflection brief substance.

She is young, this new person. A blond, wearing a black T-shirt and black jeans. As she moves towards the nurse's desk, she coughs. The sound is loud and dry, painful to Wendy's ears.

Wendy looks down at her feet, her pale-blue sneakers. The black and white floor spreads out from her like a chessboard. She hears soft voices coming from the nurse's station and it breaks through the din of elevator music.

She scans *The Barrie Examiner* resting on top a table beside her. The headline, *Police Unsure as Girl Number Five Goes Missing*, is printed in thick bold lettering and is pasted over the pictures of five young girls, all in late adolescence or early twenties. In the article, it said that the public, growing concerned, was asking the police if these disappearances were linked. In other words, was there a serial killer on the loose? The Barrie Ontario Provincial Police gave no comment, as they had not found any of the missing bodies. They promised to keep the public updated.

Again, it moves deep in the pit of her stomach.

"*Wendy.*"

The oceanic voice crashes against the shore of Wendy's eardrums, and she winces. This voice keeps her awake at night. She moves her hands to caress her swollen stomach.

"It's all right," she whispers. "There's no need to hurt Mommy here, okay?"

The strange woman turns away from the empty nurse's desk. The skin of her face and arms are milky white. Thick and black crusted gashes streak the legs of her jeans as though someone had taken a knife to them. As the strange woman smiles at her, Wendy's heart palpitates and she looks away. She thinks of the man in the blue baseball hat who has been following her for the better part of a year.

He had followed her here, to the doctor's office—always twenty or thirty yards behind. He would probably follow her home. Wendy pictures the man sitting in the café across the street, just outside of her view, sipping coffee and waiting for her appointment to end.

* * *

Seven months ago, Wendy awoke to the sound of scratching at her front door. A small sound, like a cat's claw, slow and rhythmic, scratching at wood. Wendy, lying in bed, imagined what the intruder might look like—nothing feline, but the masculine shape of a man wearing a blue baseball cap, drunk and smelling of sex. He has watched her enter and leave the apartment building for close to a month, his fiendish eyes half-closed in ecstasy. He scratched at the door now, lazily picking the lock, trying to get in quietly so as not to wake the victim.

Wendy wanted to call the police, but if they did not find the man, they would slap a fine on her for wasting their time as they had in the past. They would advise her to take a twelve-step program dealing with the young, the fat, and the raped. Victim's R' Us, or a room full of women with the same pained expression Wendy saw every morning before the mirror.

She grabbed the baseball bat she kept beside her bed, and tiptoed into the living room. Light from the hallway shone from beneath the front door from where the shadow of two feet stood waiting. The scratching was louder here, its rhythm picking up velocity as though the sick bastard on the other side sensed her approach, smelled her fear.

Taking small, furtive steps, Wendy approached the front door. She leaned close to peer through the peephole. Wind howled at her living room window, like the bellowing of lost souls. A cold draft pressed against Wendy's eye. Nobody stood on the other side. Yet, when she looked down, the pillar-like shadows remained, and the scraping continued to scratch at the frail strings of her heart.

Goose bumps rippled across her skin. Her heart beat painfully in her chest.

She raised the bat high above her shoulder and stepped back. "Go away!"

The two shadows shifted under the door. They paused, then disappeared completely. Cold wind touched Wendy's face. Perhaps she shouldn't have spoken aloud. She should have pretended she wasn't at home.

Trembling, she took a step forward, and was about to look through the peephole a second time when something slammed into the door from the other side. The force of it shook the walls, causing knickknacks sitting on shelves to crash onto the floor. It slammed again, this time causing the door to jolt from its hinges. A small, breathless scream erupted from Wendy's lips. She took a panicked step backward when the door was struck a third time, blowing it free from bolt and chain in an explosion of wooden shrapnel.

Wendy realized that she was kneeling against the back wall, holding the bat in front of her as a shield. Yellow light from beyond the front door, hanging jagged on broken hinges, illuminated the interior of her apartment, but no one stood at its threshold.

She was bleeding. Tiny wooden splinters spiked out from the flesh of her arms and the cold wind blew.

Wendy stood up. Her arms and legs stung as an icy cold sweat mingled with the blood and wooden splinters. It felt like a thousand bee stings.

She took a step forward. She had to close the front door. Why hadn't the noise aroused the curiosity of her neighbors? Another step forward and she reached out her hand.

The wind pulsed through the entryway and rattled the door, threatened to break it free from the thin threads that restrained its fall. The wind crawled and curled between her legs, entering the apartment as though it had volition of its own.

Just then, the door stood straight from its crooked stance. Wendy pulled back and the door swung violently to the right, slamming shut.

The wind from outside had stopped, its lonely howl

having gone elsewhere. In its place, she heard a ragged breath and a soft chuckle.

"Wendy!"

She stood staring at the front door, and the blood rushing through her veins turned to a strong Arctic Ocean current.

This was not the man with blue baseball hat, but something completely different.

"Wendy," it again whispered, its voice sounding like a cloud of flies hovering over a corpse.

The floor under Wendy's feet jolted as she turned around. The vision before her, a figure wearing a large black cloak, stood not five feet away. The front of its cloak opened down to its pelvis, exposing a milky white chest and stomach littered with deep, dark-red gashes. Movement jutted from where the robe joined below, thrashing and excited.

"Stop thinking of me as an 'it,'" it said. "I am most undoubtedly a he!"

With the words still ringing in Wendy's ears, the remaining crease of the creature's robe separated and unveiled the anomaly twisting and squirming from his pelvis, like a snake. Like a serpent. Grounded, Wendy could not take her eyes off it. The fear melted, her heart beating hard to a new and unfamiliar emotion.

The creature raised his arms to remove the cloak's hood. A smile of jagged sharp teeth, two slits for a nose, and two red pools on a facial landscape of white sand stared into Wendy's soul.

Smiling, his long silver teeth dug into the soft flesh of his lips and he grabbed Wendy by the arm. His hand was as cold as the winter night's wind, sending an electric chill throughout her body.

When the Serpent spoke again, there was the stench of spoiled milk and decaying vegetables.

* * *

The young woman with the blond hair and black clothes sits down in front of Wendy, blocking the view of her hollowed self. She leans back in her seat so that the backrest supports her head. Heat rushes to Wendy's cheeks, and she tries not to look at the other woman's torn pants. The woman smells like dry earth and something else Wendy cannot place.

Faint interest spreads across the woman's expression. She stares at Wendy, her bloodshot eyes unblinking, a tiny grin playing at the corners of her mouth. She sits up so suddenly that Wendy jumps in her seat, the fetal-snake twisting agony inside her gut.

"Let me guess," the woman says and places her elbows onto her knees. "About seven months or so, right?"

Wendy shakes her head, and the room grows faint with the hammering of her heart. She grips at the chair's armrests, the tips of her fingers turning white.

"Yeah, I knew you were one," the woman says and lets out a dry cough. "I wasn't certain when I came in, but now that I see you up close … yeah. The Serpent has been to you."

The snake coils and beats itself against walls of flesh, causing Wendy to tremble. "I … I don't know what you're talking about."

The woman smiles and again leans back into the chair. Her teeth are stained yellowish-brown; her eyes excited.

"You shouldn't be here," she says. "The doctor won't be able to do anything. They've no doubt run all their tests by now, right?"

Wendy wraps her arms around her bulging, oscillating stomach. "*Wendy*," the voice inside says. The deep-sea voice floods Wendy's ears, and she hunches down into her seat, her head lowered.

The strange woman's quiet chuckle breaks through residual ringing.

There are tears in Wendy's eyes. She keeps her head down and says, "I can't talk to you. Just leave me alone."

"I knew you'd say that," she says. "Listen, you're afraid. Probably think you're losing your mind."

The woman bends over, again leaning elbows on knees. She is holding a piece of paper Wendy had not noticed before.

"The Serpent came to see me, too, only a little late," the woman says, and then pauses. Her eyes linger on the - *Barrie Examiner*. "He likes women like you and me, women fated to bad men's bullshit. We are his brides, but now you are at the top of the list." She bends over, gently grabs Wendy's hand clenched at her side, and places the piece of paper into it. Her hand is cold, and although the woman has let her go, Wendy can still feel her skin tingle. "You need to remember the word written on that piece of paper. It's my name, but its *meaning* is the only thing that will save you today."

As Wendy crumples the paper in her hand, she hears the woman get up, hears soft steps leaving her alone. When she looks up, the strange woman is gone. The room is once again empty.

Wendy meets the wide-eyed expression of her ghost-like reflection and her heart pounds.

She takes the piece of paper and smoothes out its edges. Scrawled in messy handwriting and thick brownish ink is the word Hope.

"Miss Clarkson? Miss Clarkson?"

Wendy looks up. Muscles in her lower abdomen conform to the snake fetus's wishes, moving and stretching to let pass its dark, dictating form. It enters Wendy's pelvic bone, and she feels the sudden urge to urinate.

"Sorry for the wait," the nurse says. She is cradling a file under an arm. "Doctor Hamlin is back from lunch now. He is ready to see you, if you'll just follow me."

* * *

"*Wendy*!" the voice of her grandmother called from her childhood.

Her grandmother's skin had had a yellowish tinge. Her last remaining teeth blackened and crooked. Grandmother often sat on the porch, or in the kitchen, the sun shining on her dry and scabby scalp; tiny puffs of hair, tangled and unwashed, often stuck out as though made of barbed wire. Her everyday breath reeked of cigarette smoke and liquor and she always cradled a bottle of what she called her "spirits."

Filth-encrusted dishes sat scattered upon the kitchen counter, plugging the chasm of the stainless steel sink. Garbage littered the floor.

"Wendy? *Wendy*!" her grandmother shouted. "Where the fuck are you? Our guest has arrived."

At school, the other girls stuck together like a flock of birds, always giggling and squawking, cluttering the washrooms with their presence. But Wendy spent her time alone.
She feared going home. She feared the hollow abyss steadily growing somewhere deep inside her chest.

"Is she young?" a man's voice now.

"She's twelve! Young enough for you? I want the money up front, just so you know."

Wendy hid in her bedroom whenever these guests came.

This, however, always failed. Wendy knew she would be better off if she never came home from school. She knew that running away, or even telling on her grandmother, might preserve that precious something crumbling inside. But with her parents' dead and no other family, she had nowhere else to go.

"Wendy, I know you're in there!" Her grandmother stood on the other side of the door. She scratched at it slightly with a long, nicotine-withered fingernail while picking the lock. Once inside, she went to where Wendy had hidden under the bed. She reached out and grabbed her painfully by the arm.

"Don't you hide on me like that! It's time for you to earn your keep, you little slut!"
From behind Grandmother stood a man in a black suit, white shirt, red tie. He held a briefcase and a thin-lipped smile. His eyes were black, his skin milky white. Staring at her, the man whispered Wendy's name, and his smile widened.

On that day, Wendy felt the remains of whatever stood strong and proud since before the death of her parents fall like cinders. Like the temple of Self crumbling to the ground under the pressure of the stranger's weight, his mad lust-filled stare, the thrust of his hips.

* * *

Cradled in the Serpent's body on that cold winter night seven months ago, Wendy shivered. The Serpent's large erection stroked up and down upon her stomach, like a lover's tender touch. She laid on top, on her side, her legs resting between his on the couch's upholstery. His left arm held her tight, pinning her to him. The cold flesh below, raked with deep cuts, reminded Wendy of fish gills, protruding out and sinking in as he breathed. The sour stench of his seed glistened on her thighs and filled the cavity between. The stench encompassed the apartment's atmosphere like a noxious gas.

Wendy didn't mind any of this. In the Serpent's arms, she was safe. Safer than she'd ever been.

It had hurt when he was inside her—his pelvis thrusting madness against her own, the self-possessed erection filling her so completely she'd never feel alone again. But now, her skin tingled, and her sex throbbed almost pleasantly.

She had met the Serpent's gaze before climaxing, his eyes almost tender in their lust.

"No one will ever hurt you again," he had said. "Only me."

* * *

Outside, the summer's heat and humidity turns the tar and brick of downtown Barrie into wavelike phantasmagoria, mirroring the stirrings inside Wendy's heart. Not pregnant, Dr. Hamlin had said. Never will be pregnant—ovaries shriveled and dried up. When Wendy had shown him her swollen stomach, oscillating in and out, he had stammered, and mentioned a specialist he'd send her to— specializing in irritable bowel syndrome, Fibromyalgia and chronic fatigue.

The snake fetus moves as she walks, coiling and twisting deeper into her pelvis. Before leaving the doctor's office, Wendy had tried to relieve her aching bladder but to no avail. The Serpent's son had wedged itself too deep for that; blocking the minute tubing necessary.

Standing at a crosswalk, she watches the traffic pass by. Sweat soaks her hair and stings her eyes. The voice floods her ears like an echo:

"*Wendy.*"

"Hey lady, are you okay?" The deep, male voice swims through the chaos, and Wendy opens her eyes to see the sky.

When did she fall down?

"You look sick," the man continues. "You should get to the doctor."

A hand is present, and Wendy takes it. His grip is strong, and he pulls her up onto her feet with ease. He is tall with broad shoulders. His smile displays a row of crooked white teeth.

"I just came from one," Wendy replies. "He's going to send me to a specialist. Irritated bowels, or some other thing I can't remember."

The man's smile deepens; he has yet to let go of her hand.

"My name's Steve," he says, "and I think you need medical attention right now. Come on, you can barely walk."

Prisoner to Steve's hand, Wendy tries to walk away but doubles over. She watches as the sweat coagulates on her nose to drip down onto the sidewalk.

"Whoa, that's some belly you got there! Are you pregnant, or is it cancer?"

He raises her hand, pulling it around him so that she is leaning against him; his other arm supports her frail, suddenly weakened body by the waist. He rushes her down the street, where he says he has a van parked.

The pressure inside her is pushing, forcing its way out of her body. She had never felt pain like this before, the kind of pain that numbs the body, heightens the senses, and makes you shiver though covered in sweat. Once at the van, he opens the passenger door. After helping her inside, he closes the door and then studies her for a moment. He smiles, a smile Wendy has seen all too often in her life-time.

His eyes are menacing, the stubble growing on his chin thick and coarse. His baseball cap is blue and he is wearing a denim jacket and denim pants. A blue baseball cap. He is only missing the night and a dark alley.

The van is an older make, one that has no windows in the back or any chairs for people to sit on. Instead, a mat-tress, stained dark-brown in the center, covers the metal flooring. Tucked between the driver and passenger seats is a black leather bag. Wendy raises her hand and tries to escape, but the driver-side door opens, and Steve, still wearing that silly, hungry grin, enters. He closes his own door, then reaches across to strap Wendy's seatbelt across her lap and chest. "Don't want you falling out," he says, and makes no apologies at his hand brushing hard against her breasts.

"Wendy!"

The name reverberates through her eardrums, causing her vision to turn white, then black.

Opening her eyes, she looks over at Steve now driving and not showing any signs at having heard the voice. He had turned on the radio and now taps his fingers to the music's rhythm. When she rolls her head back to the pas-senger side window, she sees trees and fields passing. He had driven them out of the city—away from the hospital.

"Nice to see you back. You were gone a good five minutes." says Steve, the smile returning. His eyes are ex-cited, as though he had won the lottery.

"Where are we?" Her stomach felt as though it would burst, the Serpent's son eager to find freedom.

"Where are you taking me?"

Her questions go unanswered, the arrogant thin-lipped smile speaking volumes in the absence of words. This cannot happen to her again, especially now, of all times.

She struggles to free herself from the seatbelt, but Steve is too quick. He pulls a hunting knife he had hidden in the black leather bag. He holds the blade up to her throat, motioning for her to stop and she can see rope protruding out from inside the bag.

"You ain't going anywhere, sugar-plum."

Country music fills the silence, slow and mournful.

"You've been following me," Wendy says, her voice soft, trembling.

"I follow all my girls," he says.

The inner canal of Wendy's ear tingles as the snake fetus shifts position below. Before passing out again, she remembers the strange woman's note, the note she had thrown into the garbage while inside the doctor's office. She thought of its message, the one word that would save her today. Hope.

* * *

Wendy wakes to the sound of buzzing flies and finds this time she is outside, laying upon what feels like sticks of wood. She is on her back and dares not move. Not yet. The sun, shining high overhead, heats her face and arms. Walls of orange-yellow dirt surround her, and a thick pungent stench fills her nostrils. Once, when she was a child and living with her grandmother, a raccoon had died in the back yard. It was a baby, its belly torn with wormy intestines plugging the fatal wound. For days, it had remained rotting in the hot summer sun before anyone took it away. The stench filling the pit smells like the raccoon, only worse.

Above, Steve is whistling a jovial tune. Wendy can see the blue baseball cap floating on a bush of curly hair. He walks around the pit and drops the black leather bag at its lip. She closes her eyes and remains motionless, hoping to God that he cannot hear the madness of her heart.

For a long moment, there is silence. Then she hears the bag's zipper, and Steve's soft laughter.

"Jesus," he says, looking down at her, "I think I lucked out with you, sugar-plum. Guess you won't be trying to run for it, eh?"

Wendy opens her eyes, just slightly, to see him jump down, landing by her legs. The sound of wood snapping accompanies his fall and he stares down at her, his eyes shadowed from the visor of his cap.

"What to do with you?" he asks her unmoving body. "Thought you'd be awake by now." His eyes are thoughtful, a grin playing at the corner of his lips at all the wonderfully horrid ideas passing through his mind.

She should run, run away from this bastard, yet she remains unmoving as he kneels down between her legs. She should have never trusted him back on the street, though she didn't have much of a choice. She could barely walk. Steve closes her legs, his arms reaching to unbutton her jeans.

"Oh yeah," he says while slipping the jeans down her waist. His hands are large and strong, and he pauses to stroke her thighs, his eyes lingering. "Oh yes, such beautiful, milky-white skin."

Still holding the hunting knife, he begins to cut frantically at her jeans, tearing them off as though to satisfy primal, animal instinct. He pants and grunts in ecstasy, growing more excited at the slits he is creating across her bare legs. Although the knife hurts as it cuts, Wendy manages to remain still and quiet.

His mood shifts again once the jeans are free from flesh. His eyebrows furrow in the middle, his eyes two orbs emanating demonic rage. He cuts her underwear in two quick slices, pulls them quickly from under her, then throws his entire weight onto Wendy. He holds the knife up to her throat, leaving her arms free at her side.

"I should slit your throat and fuck your corpse!" he shouts not an inch away from her face.

Wendy, not expecting this sudden change in attack, winces. Through the open slits of her eyes, his face relaxes. An eyebrow arches. A smile replaces the mad formation of snarling, spitting lips and teeth.

He remains on top of her, and Wendy can feel the beginnings of an erection building inside his pants.

"So, you were awake, huh?"

He doesn't give her time to answer. His head lowers to lick, kiss, and then bite her lips and tongue. Wendy tastes coppery blood filling her mouth, her own blood. His grip on the hunting knife at her neck tightens, and his free hand reaches down between them, unfastening his own pants.

He pulls back his head. With his mouth dripping with Wendy's blood, he says, "I like it better when they're awake."

When Wendy wiggles, trying to find a way out, the snake fetus moves and she cries out in pain. *Protect me!* the oceanic voice says. Steve looks down upon her, his face large and sick with her blood. He smiles, thinking he is the culprit of her suffering. His erect penis is in his hand and he is trying to enter her, but something is blocking the way.

"You're … not … getting away with this," Wendy hisses. "I'll kill you … I'll fucking kill you!"

"I'd like to see ... how," he is grunting in the effort of both controlling her movements and trying to enter her ... "just how you'd accomplish that."

Wendy answers by wrapping her legs around his waist, her arms around his back. Hugging tightly onto him, she can't see his face, only his neck. His throbbing jugular.

Wendy shifts her weight and digs her teeth deep into his flesh, tearing through skin and arteries. The force of the blood is like a waterfall and gushes into her mouth, down her throat, and Steve screams. At the same time, the Serpent's son viciously tears at the inner walls of her birth canal. Her own screams through torn skin and blood are a horrid gurgling sound and she thrusts Steve's weight so that she is now on top, their bodies tangled and joined as one.

The would-be rapist tries to use the knife, but Wendy rips her head back, dangling crimson meat from her bared teeth, and he loses his grip. She spits the meat from her mouth, and grabs at the knife dangling uselessly by the open wound at his throat—his hand that had held the knife now failing at blocking the flow of blood.

Steve whimpers, calls Wendy a bitch, but he is weakening.

Wendy picks up the knife, and feels a rush of energy. She raises the knife and brings it down. It slices through his cheek and possibly his tongue, but this does not matter. She lifts the knife free as she releases her grip on him, letting his body free of hers. She brings the knife down again, this time penetrating his collarbone.

Steve's screams are gurgled just as hers had been moments ago. His eyes roll up into his head and his body trembles violently as Wendy again brings the knife down, this time in the gut.

She slices at his body as though it represents every single man who had touched her in the wrong way, as though it were a grandmother prostituting an orphaned child instead of nurturing her, loving her. She rips and tears at the body until the convulsions stop and he lays unmoving.

His corpse stares at the sky, his body covered in blood. Wendy almost laughs; Steve is still holding his erect penis in his other hand. Semen mixes in with the mess. But her laughter is cut short. Arms and legs jut out from beneath Steve's corpse, adding a strange, almost godlike appearance to the would-be rapist. Her eyes scan the small terrain of the pit, the blood in her veins going cold, and despite the heat of the day, the skin on her arms ripple into goose bumps.

A whimper escapes her throat, and she jumps back until she reaches the pit's wall, and slams into something cold and hard. She turns around and falls back to a sitting position. She cannot fathom that she is sitting on the corpse of a murderer and his victims. Her eyes concentrate on the site before her. Another body, crumpled in the corner, wearing a black T-shirt with black jeans torn around her knees and ankles. Her hair was blond, but now caked brown in dry blood. The pale-white skin of her face has turned black; it holds the expression of terror absent from the doctor's waiting room, where Wendy had met her. Hope's body is days old, if not weeks, and Wendy wonders why she didn't recognize her as the young woman whose face was added to the missing persons file plastered all over the local press.

Jolts of sharp pain explode from down below. Wendy crawls to the other side of the pit and climbs out. On the surface, there is a dirt road, a long and twisting driveway, and a small, dilapidated farmhouse. She falls onto her back, her face covered in blood and sweat and agony. The snake fetus wants out, and when she peels her eyes away from the sky to look down between her legs, she sees its ambition in the form of two stubby arms reaching out of her, pulling itself free.

Then, sudden release. It is out of her and lying wiggling on the ground. The baby is nothing like a snake, but plump and grey-white with clots of red plastered all over it. His penis is large and moves of its own accord, its head bulbous. His eyes are the black holes Wendy imagined they might be, much like his father's. She does not doubt that they glow crimson in the dark.

The Serpent's son does not cry, just stares. At Wendy.

She feels tears on her cheeks. They are not the tears of sadness she is accustomed to, but of a joy Wendy had never before felt. She feels complete, somehow, holding the baby's dark gaze. Although the Serpent had seeded this little creature, it belongs to her now. This is *her* son, the Serpent's gift. Hope for the future.

* * *

"You have a strong spirit," the Serpent had told her seven months ago while she laid on top his cold, snake-like body. "It is buried deep somewhere inside of you, but it is not dead. You only need the seeds to help wake her up, set her free, and nobody will hurt you ever again."

The Seminary

The poster was yellow with bold black lettering and a picture; a silhouette showing what looked like a young man wearing makeup, stripes running from his eyes down through his nose, cheeks and mouth in swirls. He was screaming up at the sky, his hand held up with clenched fingers. On his chest rested a necklace with an inverted cross. Above the picture were the words, "The Seminary," and below it a date and an address.

"The Seminary," Alicia said. "Huh, must be a new band or something."

"How do you know it's a band?" Dan said. "It could be anything. It doesn't say."

Alicia rolled her eyes and inhaled deeply. "Well, whatever it is, it's tonight. And I wanna check it out."

"I thought we were gonna have a peaceful night at home."

Again, Alicia rolled her eyes and let go of his hand. "That's all you ever want to do. If I left it up to you, we'd never leave the fuckin' apartment."

Dan shrugged. What was he to say? She was right. There was more than enough useless things to entertain you in your own home. Tonight he had planned on getting a strong buzz and throwing a horror movie into the DVD.

But if he brought that up, Alicia would probably say that that's all he ever wanted to do as well.

Alicia looked up at him, her face down so that her black hair nearly covered her pale cheeks. She stuck out her bottom lip, a thick wet worm.

Dan sighed. "Jesus! I never get my way."

Alicia squealed. "I knew you'd cave," she said. "And you *always* get your way. Now it's my turn."

Whatever, Dan thought. But something did not sit right with him about this. Perhaps it was that face on the poster or its lack of information, or maybe it was Alicia thinking he had agreed to go without his actually having done so, but his guts twisted at the thought of going. When he looked at Alicia, however, she was looking up at him with her big eyes. She grabbed his hand into both of hers and smiled.

It was too late to argue.

"Well, we'd better get going if we want to be on time," he said. "Whatever it is, it starts in about an hour."

* * *

"Only those who have sinned come here!" A homeless man with a large beard and a ragged long coat screamed. He stood in front of an abandoned-looking warehouse, holding a beat up leather-bound book to the sky. When he laughed it sounded insane. The entire presence of the man reeked of madness.

"Ah fuck," Dan said. "I bet he stinks like a dumpster."

"Don't be so negative," Alicia said.

"But he's standing at the end of the line."

"All will suffer the wrath of our Lord and Savior, Jesus Christ!" the homeless man screamed. "And I will have my *revenge*!"

Dan and Alicia edged their way closer, keeping their distance from the homeless guy. The people in front of him, punks wearing torn denim pants and coats, their hair spiked into great, multicolored Mohawks, glared over their shoulders, their fists clenched. Maybe Dan and Alicia wouldn't have anything to worry about, if the homeless guy kept up this litany. But the punks didn't make a move. Instead, they turned back around and lit a thick, home-rolled cigarette. Within seconds, the pungent scent of marijuana filled Dan's nostrils, and he closed his eyes, hoping to catch a whiff.

"I didn't know punks were into black metal," Alicia said.

"Huh?"

"Those guys ahead of the homeless dude," she said, pointing. "What are *they* doing here? The Seminary is obviously a black metal band."

"We don't know that The Seminary *is* a band or that *this* is a concert," Dan reminded her. "The poster didn't say."

"What else *could* it be, dickhead?" Alicia said, scowling at him.

Sighing, Dan shook his head and looked away. In front of them, the homeless guy was staring at them, at *him*, his eyes wide, a large smile showing off brown and black teeth.

"God has seen the likes of you in the hearts of men," the homeless guy said. His smile disintegrated as he spoke, his face turning red under the harsh streetlights as he motioned with one hand to the warehouse. "*This* is your judgment! I know how you will fare."

"Then why are you here, freakazoid?" Dan said.

The smile returned to the homeless guy's face. "It's my right to go wherever I please," he said. "Especially if it don't cost anything. At least, I don't think it did last time."

"My God," Alicia said. "Stop talking to us. You're a fuck-ing hypocrite."

"Hell will devour *your* soul tonight, little girl," he said. "But for me, I will be triumphant."

The homeless man then thrust his leather bound Bible into the air and, looking beyond Dan and Alicia, restarted his litany to the growing crowd. Behind them, the line had grown considerably, and Dan wondered where they had all come from. They could not have all seen the same poster that he and Alicia had. What surprised Dan the most, how-ever, were the different types of people who had come. There were many Goths, just like he and Alicia, wearing black leather and corpse makeup, but there were also preps, emos, rappers, and old people even. All of them looked around at their surroundings as though confused at how they had gotten here.

The unsettled feeling Dan had felt earlier in his guts re-turned like a fist to his stomach. Something was wrong here. But when he brought up the issue to Alicia, she just looked at him as though his skin had suddenly turned green and grown scales.

"You're fuckin' paranoid," she said. "Honestly, some-times I don't know why I'm with you."

The line began to move with sighs of relief coming from the people immediately around the homeless guy. Two figures stood by the entrance, both wearing brown robes, where a new stench introduced itself, overwhelming the weed and the homeless guy's body odor. The stench was familiar. Dan had only been outside the city once before, on a school field trip to the middle of nowhere. "What you're smelling," Mrs. Dawson, Dan's teacher, said to a class holding their noses and looking ready to vomit, "is manure, which is used in fields, such as this one, as ferti-lizer."

Manure, Dan thought. *What the hell's going on here?*

"This is gonna be awesome," Alicia said as they crossed the threshold. The robes of the two figures standing by the entrance looked as though they were threaded from straw. The figures themselves held wooden staffs at their sides. Dan gaped at all the hair covering their hands and forearms, their fingers likewise with long, uncut nails. And from beneath the hoods, of which Dan could see only darkness, came a soft, nearly inaudible pig-like snorting.

Awesome indeed, Dan thought. He wanted to laugh sarcasm into Alicia's face. The dread intensified with each step he took, leading him, leading them *all*, into a great cavern of the unknown. He looked back at the pig men guarding the entrance, then back at Alicia. He could not leave her here. Not amongst the pig men with their hairy hands and staffs. Not with the homeless guy and his Bible.

"Come on," he said, "we're getting out of here." He grabbed Alicia's hand, ignored her loud protests, and headed back towards the entrance. Something then pressed up hard against his chest, stopping him. A hairy, long finger-nailed hand, smelling strongly of the pigs and cows of his long ago field trip, was planted over his heart. A voice, raspy as it was angry, said, "Turn around. The Band's about to go on stage. You don't want to miss it."

"Let me through," Dan said, but the hands curled into a fist, crunching up his Cradle of Filth T-shirt. The hand then thrust him forward, closer to the foul smelling robed figure.   "You cannot leave once you've entered," the voice rasped, its breath a foul mixture of rotting meat and sulfa. The hand pushed, the fingers letting go, and Dan staggered backwards, nearly knocking Alicia over.

"Thank God," she said once she had efficiently patted the wrinkles straight on her skirt. "You can leave if you want, but I'm staying, you asshole!" Then, after a silence, she added, "Told you it was a band."

The stench of manure only grew stronger as they turned back around and entered the great blackness. Their feet kicked at the straw scattered across the cement floor, making soft swishing sounds as they walked.

"Are you trying to tell me that you see nothing odd going on here?"

Alicia sighed, her bottom teeth jutting out and her eyes scanning the upper parts of her eye sockets. When she spoke, it was as though to a child. "This is a concert. A *heavy metal* concert. Everything you see here are props. Now if you'd just relax, you might enjoy yourself."

Inhaling deeply, Dan once more took in his surroundings. Large torches lay at forty-five degree angles from sconces on the walls, to the right was a bar with two bartenders working busily at the growing crowd, and at the far end of the warehouse, a stage, at least six feet high. Above the stage, purple lights illuminated a drum kit, amps and guitars, a keyboard.

A concert indeed.

Still strange, though. He'd never heard of The Seminary, yet with a get-up like this, they had to be making some money. That, or one of the band members came from a rich family.

His heart began to settle, though. Everything looked as it should be. A concert. He and Alicia had found themselves at a free concert, and that was all there was to it. He should be happy, content, not this panic frenzied loser.

Alicia smiled at him, the first true smile he'd seen from her since they arrived. "It's okay," she said, and laughed. "You just read too many horror stories."

* * *

The homeless guy continued to shout, shooting his hand and the Bible into the air. His voice often carried over the noise of the crowd, crying about revenge and punishment.

Dan and Alicia did their best to avoid the man. Nobody in their right mind would want to get stuck next to him in the mosh pit.

"Don't you think this is strange?" Dan said, looking around at the crowd.

"You're not loosing yourself again, are you?"

"No, but it's friggin' packed in here, Alicia. Look around."

Alicia did. She then looked up at him and shrugged. "So?"

"Have you ever heard of The Seminary before tonight?"

Alicia tilted her head in thought. When she looked back up at him, she shook her head. "What the fuck does it matter? It's a free concert. Of course people are gonna show up."

But, most of these people don't look like they'd be interested in what was depicted on the poster, he added to himself. The man with long hair, screaming up into the sky with splayed and clenched fingers and an inverted cross hanging from his neck could only mean one subgenre from the heavy metal scene. Black metal. Yet, just as with outside in the line-up, inside the crowd was quite eclectic. Men and women looking like college professors walked beside kids in ragged clothing and spiked hair. Senior citizens with thick glasses and sweaters stood next to pale-faced Goths. All stood as close to the stage as possible and waited, their eager talk a constant murmur.

Calm down, Dan told himself. *It's just a concert. Nothing else.*

But there was something wrong going on here. He just knew it, and was about to grab Alicia's attention again to tell her when the lights from above dimmed, and the stage lights grabbed his attention. One of the pig men from the entrance was up there, walking with his grizzly hands folded before him. He stepped up to the microphone, and with one hairy and long-nailed finger, he tapped the edge of it. The sound echoed from the speakers throughout the warehouse, and the audience cheered.

"*Silence*," he said, its voice as gravely, as animalistic as it was at the front door when Dan had tried to escape, only amplified a hundred times.

When the audience had settled, the pig man continued.

"You are all here tonight to celebrate what you are!" Again, the crowd cheered, fists rising into the air. Instead of yelling at the audience to silence, the robed figure waited, only continuing when the cheers became a murmur. "Tonight you will know what color paints the flesh beneath your skin. You will know if you have bricks or shit inside the walls of your skull. Tonight you will be nothing but what you already are: a beast, a monster. *Human*!"

As the audience cried out, thrusting fists into the air, Dan wondered what it was about the robed figure's words that riled everyone up so much. All around him people were screaming, their skin turning red, veins popping out on their necks and faces. Even Alicia seemed enraged, her mouth stretched open, her teeth looking almost like sharpened points, her eyes like wrinkled hollow sockets.

"I give you," the robed figure screeched over the roar of the crowd. "I give you, The Seminary!"

Sudden noise exploded, drowning out the audience. Like chainsaws, the music shredded through the audience, a sonic pulse that pumped against Dan's chest. The crowd pushed forward, shoving Dan against those who stood before him. And from above, up on the stage, a mass of hair wind-milling circles or violently flapping up and down, the five members of The Seminary had their instruments in hand and were bouncing around like the demons they so obviously wanted to portray. They wore black leather with spikes jutting out from their wrists and ankles. On their faces, the typical corpse paint of a black metal band.

A concert after all. One like many both Dan and Alicia had gone to together many times. But there *was* something wrong with this one. In all the concerts Dan had been to in his life, and there were many, he never once seen old women crowd surfing, or old men jabbing people in the face with their elbows, all in a rage and lost in the music. But that was exactly what Dan was looking at, not five feet away, right in the thick of the mosh pit. Something didn't add up, and if he were lucky enough, he and Alicia wouldn't be here long enough to find out what was going on.

* * *

Dan grabbed Alicia by the elbow between songs and pulled her towards him. Over by the front doors, however, there were more of the pig men, standing with hands folded before them, their heads bowed. There had to be another way out of here, an old warehouse such as this. He only had to find it.

"Let me go, you asshole!" Alicia screamed. She shook her elbow, forcing Dan to let go. Glaring at him, she turned back around just as the band started its next song. A man wearing a black wife beater with long black hair splayed over his muscular shoulders stepped between him and Alicia. He shook his head and, when he smiled, Dan would have sworn that he'd seen the other man's eyes glow a deep crimson, like the burning embers of a fire pit.

"Alicia!" Dan yelled. "We've got to leave. It isn't safe!" But it was useless. The buzz saw music cut right through the sound of his voice.

Alicia raised her arms, her fists jutting out her fore and pinky fingers in the horn gesture. Dan tried to move to his left then his right, trying to get to her, but Mr. Muscles blocked his every move. He stared down at Dan, the smile unmoved, the glowing ember of his eyes burning dark and ominous light. Despite the people surrounding him, he felt cold, colder than he'd ever been in his life. He looked back, the robed figures were walking away from the entryway towards the crowd. Now, if he could only get a hold of Alicia, he could get them out.

The song ended and the singer addressed the crowd.

"You guys are fucking insane!" he shouted to the crowd's delight. When they calmed down, he continued. "This next song is what you most of you came for," his said, his voice lowered almost to a snarl. "With it, you will find yourselves where you've always dreamed to be. Between heaven and hell, between anguish and ecstasy, this is your *Descent from Faith*!"

This was it. Dan had to get to Alicia. And both of them had to leave. Now. The opening notes were already blasting through the warehouse. Dan ducked and pushed himself forward with all he had and managed to slip around Mr. Muscles' left arm. He slammed into Alicia's back, grabbed her by the shoulders, and tried to pull her to his left, through the crowd and away from Mr. Muscles.

But the other man was far too quick.

A hand gripped Dan's shoulder from behind. It turned him around. He then had just enough time to see Mr. Muscles' upraised fist as it smashed into his face, knocking his head back, causing stars to shoot across his vision. His legs gave out from beneath him and he fell hard onto his ass. The mass of flesh surged all around him, all moving towards the stage, trying to suffocate him, squish him like a bug. He struggled, forcing the muscles in his legs, some of which he never had to use before, to stand, but there were just too many people. He was stuck. He would die here, a failure.

Hands forced their way under his armpits, and Dan was suddenly thrust upwards. An overwhelming smell of body odor, piss and dried whiskey flooded Dan's nostrils.

"The fight ain't over yet," the homeless man said into Dan's ear. He was surprised he could even hear it. "It's only just begun."

With one dirt-encrusted finger, the homeless man pointed at the audience before them, then up at the stage, where the band was thrashing around like wild beasts. The guitarist tossed his head up, his long hair flung at his back, and Dan's heart nearly stopped. *Things* moved beneath the man's skin, thick and long like worms. He opened his mouth, and his gums bulged as his teeth grew longer and sharper, the entire jaw shifting in its hinges, becoming thicker, bulgier. If there was no music, no crowd to drown it out, Dan knew he'd hear the bones snapping and crackling, like stepping on sticks in the park.   All other members of the band were likewise changing, the singer standing in the middle. He raised a finger as he chanted to the audience:

Under a blood-red moon
We feed the desire
And the earth becomes our flesh
Rivers our blood
To split the moon
And find what's at the end

The crowd surged around Dan, pushing and prodding him. Even over the music he could hear their snarls, their screams, the popping and cracking of their metamorphosing bones. The skin and muscle surrounding him was convulsing, violently trembling. Skulls contorted into new shapes, jaws and teeth becoming abnormally large. No two were the same. The only similarity was their clothes tearing free from their new shapes. That, and they all began to tear at the ones who had not changed.

Fighting the crowd, Dan tried to push his way back to Alicia. He could see her face, her eyebrows wrinkled together, her mouth opened wide. It almost looked sexual, her facial expression, and Dan, remembering who had been standing behind her, pushed as hard as his aching muscles would allow.

Her face came closer, closer, and behind her, still wearing the black wife beater, but otherwise in the midst of his own change, was the man who had punched him in the face. He held Alicia by the shoulders with two massive hands, the nails long and black, the fingers bony despite their size. The skin of his mouth stretched over teeth too big for its face. They looked like winter icicles, his teeth. His black eyes were sunken deep into their sockets. Horns were growing out from his forehead, black like crude oil yet somehow they seemed to soak in the lights from above, which had at some point turned back on. But he was still changing, growing bigger and bigger. *A pink demon*, Dan thought. *A demon stretching and warping human flesh to its own design.*

He almost laughed, but the crowd separated at his front for a moment, and Dan noticed that the pink demon was no longer wearing pants. It was holding the hem of Alicia's skirt up over her back while she held her naked ass end against its pelvis. Its thrust made her thighs jiggle like jelly, and now that Dan was closer, he could hear screams of pleasure.

"No!"

He was so close now, so *fucking* close, and yet so far away. Alicia opened her eyes, and when she noticed him, the horror no doubt painted across his face, she smiled. The music pounded from the stage, an abstract sound that made no real sense, or perhaps it was the audience, in their new form, screaming high-pitched and insane in their torture and pleasure. All of them, he noticed now, all of them but him were engaged in similar acts as Alicia. Gone from the humans were the old, the punks, the blue-collar workers. All that was left were the Goths, the metal heads who wanted a good show. A good show they were getting. All but Dan, who was too busy pushing himself towards Alicia, pushing and pushing, but he was too skinny, too weak, and those blocking the way to powerful.

The creature behind Alicia was double its original form, triple. Alicia grimaced as the pink demon violently pounded her from behind. Her eyes rolled up and she opened her mouth again, but this time blood poured out with chunks of wet red that followed, as though she were vomiting parts of her insides out. Her body went slack, and the pink demon roared, pulling her body free from his and it held her tight against his massive body. Her body looked like a child's compared to the pink demon's, and it held her towards Dan, as though to say, "Is this what you wanted?"

Her lifeless body sagged in its grip, her eyes open, staring at nothing, blood drenching the front of her blouse, soaking her naked legs.

"No!"

He never had a chance. Her body came crashing down on his head, and he fell back. Her body flapped upon the audience like a rag doll. The people ... Dan blinked ... the *things* surrounding him raised her body up high, adding their own broken humans to the fore while their claws, there was no other word for what used to be human nails, dug into flesh. They were going to tear Alicia's and all other bodies apart.

With the demons' attention on them, he bent down and squirmed through their twisted legs and torsos. The floor, now covered in blood, stuck to his boots and sometimes he slipped and nearly fell. Somehow, he managed to stay up, and finally, he found the end to this horrifying mass of flesh. A small opened area, where he could crouch amongst the dead lying there and wait for this horror to end. If it ever would.

The music stopped, and the band, bloodthirsty, flesh-starved, dived into the swarming crowd in a spray of blood.

Dan, covered in blood and God only knew what else, crawled to the wall where others, all dead no doubt, waited. Dan no longer cared. Up ahead, the homeless man lay sprawled out, his ribs and intestines exposed and glistening in the dim lighting, his eyes, like Alicia's, staring up at nothing. He had managed to cling to his Bible the whole time, a miracle at last, and Dan pried it from the man's fingers before crawling away. The Bible hadn't helped the poor bastard, but it might him.

All I can do is hope and pray, he thought as he crawled towards the entrance. It became a mantra, and soon he was saying it aloud.

"All I can do is hope and pray. All I can do is hope and pray. All I can do is hope ..."

* * *

"... and pray."

The demons filled Dan's view, their skin rippled with muscle, their cocks, very much like the one that had killed Alicia, thick and large and erect like baseball bats. Drenched in blood and with no humans left, they tore at each other with their claws and teeth, doing no real damage. Dan wondered why they didn't just turn their rage onto the city.

Perhaps it's just part of their Satanic ritual, Dan thought, and he laughed.

"If hell exists, then so does heaven," he said aloud and laughed even harder.

But he had to keep quiet, or the demons would see him, and they'd know that he knew of their secret. That they lived by night and day as humans, held real jobs like most, or perhaps toured in a band like The Seminary, but in reality—*reality*! how funny that idea alone was—in reality they were monsters. Monsters from hell, Satan spawn, living-breathing-walking-nightmares!

Dan clutched the Bible close to his chest. He tried to stop the laughter, but could not. His chest convulsed with it, filling the growing silence of the warehouse. The demons had settled down; they were now heading for the main entrance, some of them changed back into old men and women, the young and the middle-aged, some no doubt the blue-collared workers of before. It was hard to tell, they were all naked.

Some of them were looking at him. One was Mr. Muscles, the demon who'd killed his Alicia. Stepping over severed arms and legs, the demon approached Dan and knelt down. Back in his human form, he looked no less threatening. But he smiled at Dan, wiping the blood, *Alicia's* blood, from his sagging dick and licking it off his fingers.

"Sorry about your girlfriend," he said. "She tastes real nice, but I'm sure you already know that."

Dan held the Bible out before him and the demon's smile disintegrated. He sneered and stood up to leave. Another demon stepped up beside him.

"Another survivor, huh?"

"Yeah. Real loony bin material, too."

The stench of smoke brought Dan to his feet. Fires climbed the wall near where the stage was. Some of the men and women carried instruments with them as they left, naked and indifferent to Dan stepping between them.

Still, Dan giggled. Holding the Bible with white-pressed fingers, he giggled and pointed.

"You're all demons!" he shouted. "If hell exists—and I have seen proof of it tonight!—then so does heaven!"

None paid him any mind, however. Their eyes were heavy with exhaustion, and they all seemed eager to leave, now that the old warehouse was on fire. Outside, there was a truck full of clothes and water. There the demons gathered, washing themselves, then dressing.

Dan turned back and headed to where the homeless man slept his eternal sleep. He knelt down beside him, and with two fingers, closed the man's staring eyes.

"I should have listened to you," he said. "Every time I tried to leave, they wouldn't let me. I've lived a life of sin, my brother. And yet tonight I was spared judgment!"

His laughter made his throat raw and his lungs burn. He had to leave soon. The fire was getting closer, its smoke nearly suffocating.

Reaching down, he pulled the homeless man's coat off and wrapped it around his own shoulders. Long and thick, it looked like it would do well in both summer and winter in protecting him from the elements. He had a job to do now, and he needed all the protection he could find.

"I've got your Bible and coat," he said. "I hope you don't think of it as stealing. I mean, you don't need it anymore, do you?" He giggled, but it died with the next thought, and he felt his eyes water.

"I didn't even know your name."

He stood up, propped the Bible out before him, and headed outside into the chill night air.

* * *

The afternoon was sweltering. Sweat soaked the clothes inside his long coat, but he barely even noticed.

"Demons roam the earth, my friends," he yelled, but nobody was listening. "I have seen them with my own eyes. And if we don't fight them, God's judgment will be swift and brutal. For our God is as jealous and unforgiving as he is loving!" He held the good book out at his front, as though offering proof. But, as usual, the people just passed by. They didn't even look at him. Some dropped change into his morning coffee.

He smiled. It was like this every day. Rain, sunshine, or snow, people just did not want to hear the truth. What they didn't know was that their ignoring him only made him want to try even harder.

"Demons, I say!" he shouted. "They want to consume your flesh, your very soul! And I—"

A hand touched his shoulder from behind, its iron grip silencing him. But there was something else. Something that made his stomach twist. A feeling he hadn't felt since … since …

"What is your name, child?"

The voice rattled, and the hand on his shoulder clenched, turned him around to face the speaker. He was an old man, his face one massive wrinkle. He wore a long coat that hid his hands.

"Wha … what?"

"I said, what is your name, child?"

He remembered something from long ago: black clothes and makeup, loud music, drugs, alcohol, and a woman with black hair who never listened to him. Even so, the thought of her, the *reminder* of her made his eyes water. He then remembered death, of bodies changed and contorted. He remembered smoke. But all that was from a different life. A life that had died. He shook his head.

"I am The Preacher," he said.

The old man squinted up at him. Either his lips spread into a smile or a snarl, The Preacher wasn't sure.

"They're coming back," the old man said. And he raised an arm, one hairy finger with a long, curled and yellow fingernail, pointing across the street where a man in overalls was gluing a poster to the brick wall.

It was a yellow poster. From here, The Preacher could read the words, The Seminary.He turned to the old man with the familiar hands, but he was gone.

No matter. The Preacher smiled. He'd been waiting for this moment for a long, long time. This was a message from God himself. He would finally allow his faithful servant his revenge.

The Preacher skipped across the street, laughing and dodging cars as he went. The show would no doubt be tonight. How he knew this, The Preacher wasn't entirely certain, but he knew it as fact. All he needed was an address, of which the poster would supply. And it did, right at the bottom, beneath the picture of a man outlined in black screaming at the sky.

"A new day has arrived, my children," he said to those immediately closest to him. He pointed to the cluster of posters, and for once, people stopped to look. "Judgment for all who go! But I will seek my revenge!"

Soon, there was a crowd. They were all finally interested in what he had to say.

He raised his hands to the sky.

"Hallelujah!" he said. "Hallelujah!"

The Witch at Midnight

Sammy looks at the moon, fat and silver in the cloudless sky. She hears a voice, her grandmother, saying, "The Goddess! She shifts our oceans, changes people into things they didn't know existed within them. Can you feel its power, child?"

"No, Nana," she lies. The silver penetrates her skin. It paints the ground beneath her feet and the hills and trees surrounding them. It is the most beautiful thing she has ever seen, and it threatens to steal her breath away, like it does every night like tonight. She wants to howl at it, to get down on all fours and scream in joy and celebration until her throat burns and its blinding silver light is out of her like the possessive phantom it is, simply so it can possess her again, this time sending Sammy onto the damp dewy grass in pure exhaustion. She would then close her eyes and sleep, bathed in warm liquid grey.

Nana can hear the lie in her voice. Or perhaps it's that she can see it in her facial expression. Sammy doesn't know, but Nana's laughter sounds like rocks clacking together.

"You're older now," she says, "so you're better at hiding it. But I know the truth. I can see it in you."

Hands touch her from behind. Above, clouds of which

Sammy had not noticed before move in. They look like smoke as they pass by the moon.

"Although you are still young," Nana says. "And you have a lot to learn. I envy you your youth and innocence. Maybe one day you will get to be as old as I am. Maybe. We shall see, won't we?"

The hands turn her around, and Nana is looking down at her with her small eyes that are lost to shadow so that her face looks like a skull with flabby, wrinkled cheeks. Somewhere off in the distance, there is a rumble of thunder, and Sammy can smell rain on the air.

"Come with me, child," Nana says. "It's time for you to find out who you are."

Her grandmother grabs her by the wrist and guides her toward the woods, toward the shadow that lies deep within.

"Shouldn't we head back? Nana? I think it's going to rain soon."

"A storm *is* coming. It's coming for you. And for me."

Sammy had never heard her Nana speak like this before, using these types of words. Almost threatening. The grip on her wrist tightens. Sammy's heart pounds inside her chest as they enter the pitch black of the forest. Somehow, this darkness feels like death, like something complete and irreversible. Sammy takes in deep breaths, lets Nana guide her.

After all, the old woman wouldn't hurt her. Would she? She never had before. Sammy knew that her grandmother was a little strange, with her talk of magic, her altars, plants, potions, and pentacles. But the old woman's eccentricities had never bothered Sammy.

Until tonight.

Think happy thoughts, she demands of herself. *Think happy thoughts and this will go away.*

Nana is still there, still dragging her through the inky forest. Somehow the old woman can find her way through the maze of trees and avoid their sharp wooden fingers. Even though she is guiding Sammy, the branches scratch at her own skin as she passes by. Sticks snap and crack beneath her weight, yet her Nana makes no sound. She wouldn't even know that the old woman was even there if not for the cold, iron grip around her small, fragile wrist.

Deeper they go, walking forever, it seems, and Sammy wonders if it will ever stop. Maybe next time Mom and Dad want to get rid of her for the weekend, she'll tell them no. She's not going anywhere near Nana again.

The rocks of Nana's lungs clack together in laughter as though the old woman can read her thoughts. She tries to pull away, but the grip only tightens, and she wonders if it might be a good idea to scream for help.

But there's nobody around. Not for miles and miles. That's what her mother always said when reflecting of her own childhood in these hills. How lonely and secluded it was. How boring.

She opens her mouth to scream anyway, if only to release the anxiety, when the silver of the moon returns, and Nana stops her frantic walk forward. Sammy slams into her back. The old woman barely moves.

They are at a large clearing. Directly at the center, there is what appears to be an old fire pit; she can't tell for sure, in the dim light it looks like a black hole. A small table sits before it, a knife at its center. It reminds Sammy of the altar back at Nana's home, the one with the pentacle drawn on the table cloth.

Nana lets go of her hand. Sammy rubs at the spot, now itchy, as though the very touch of the old woman is diseased. Brilliant white light flashes. A thick rumble from the sky quickly follows. Her Nana was at the fire pit, almost naked looking in the lightning. Now, in the darkness, there are more quick flashes—the flick of Nana's lighter—and then a fire. A fire pit, after all, and the fire grows and grows. Nana kneels at the edge of the pit, opposite the altar, her cheeks expanding, smoothing out the wrinkles, her breath feeding the fire.

Leaves and tree branches rustle with the wind, and when the lightning flashes again, the fire soaks in some of its severity.

"Come over here, child," her Nana says. "I want to show you something."

The fire is quite large now. The adolescent flames lick above the logs her grandmother had stacked within the pit. They lick at the sky in a spastic dance. Sammy doesn't want to move. Knows that something is wrong with this place, with her grandmother. Wasn't it stuff like this that the people of her church warned her about? She always knew, of course, that Nana called herself a witch, but ... how true was it? Until now, Sammy had always thought that the woman was joking. Trying to scare her with her candles, pentagrams, and altars.

If it never scared her before, it most certainly does now. Yet, if she were to turn and run, where would she go? They'd walked for what felt like hours. Even her feet, used to running at school, felt blistered.

"Come here, child," Nana repeats. "I won't hurt you. Not to worry. But, you're old enough now to figure out where you belong in this world. You've almost had your first bleeding, after all. But before that happens, I want to show you your roots, where you come from."

She holds out her hand. She still stands at the other end of the fire, opposite the altar. From here, the glow of the fire makes her face look even more so like a skull with fleshy, wrinkled cheeks.

"I'm your grandmother, child. Do you really think I'd hurt you?"

Sammy slowly makes her way to the other side of the fire. She takes Nana's hand, which is still shockingly cold, despite the fire. The moon is once again gone from the sky, a thick blackness up there to replace it. Forks of lightning reach across that abyss, and the wind picks up, blowing cool air at the fire, blowing Nana's long, grey hair across her face. She doesn't notice as she looks down, smiling, at her granddaughter.

"Though the moon may be our Goddess, the Earth is our *true* Mother," she says. "Everything we can see and touch, and those we cannot, belong of this world, of this universe. Even we humans crawled out from its mud, and it's our destiny to return to it."

Nana again lets go of Sammy's wrist. It itches as before, so she rubs it while Nana walks around to the other side of the fire until she is standing behind the altar. She lifts knife that is there high into the air and turns around.

"Mother North," she calls, her voice louder and more demanding than Sammy had ever heard from her. "I call upon you to sanctify and protect from evil our blessed circle. Come forth now, and welcome!"

Nana walks in a circle around the fire, stopping at east and west and south, calling for the guardians of their respective points. When she is back at the altar, she holds both hands to the sky, the knife, painted black and glowing in the firelight. Her smile is wide, her eyes wide with reverence and awe.

Can she see something I can't? Sammy wonders.

"They have come," Nana whispers. The wind brings new sounds with it, of sticks snapping in the woods surrounding them, of grunts and snarls. When Sammy looks, she can see shadows moving out there within the frequent flashes of lightning. Inhuman, and yet human, shapes with two arms and two massive legs bent the wrong way. Horns atop their heads. Something large protruding from between their legs.

And … is that laughter?

Sammy's skin prickles with gooseflesh, her heart pounds as sweat beads on her forehead. She has never been so afraid in her life, yet there is Nana, smiling like some old crone, a witch at midnight with all the dark powers of the world on her side, missing only a cauldron and a pointy hat.

"Evil is only a matter of opinion, child," Nana says. "Evil is also the forcing of harm upon another for no reason at all but your own pleasure. I have never intentionally hurt anyone or anything in my life without reason. I am not evil. And neither are you. You know this, deep down, Sammy. All you have to do is look."

Rain begins to pelt at their skin. It stings, as though tiny rocks fly at her. Nana doesn't seem to notice.

"The Mother does not care for evil or good," she continues. "Neither does our Goddess the moon, or the God of the sun. Nature does not hurt with pleasure, with the intention to simply hurt and nothing more. And I do not do this to hurt you, but to show you what I am talking about."

Nana raises the black knife to her side, the point of its blade at the edge of her throat. She then pushes, and the knife slides in deep. Sammy screams as she watches a spurt of blood squirt over the altar. But Nana only pushes the knife in deeper, dragging it across the front of her throat until it is nothing but a black-crimson mouth of its own. Blood gushes down Nana's chest, squirting into the fire, where it hisses and a separate, blacker smoke rises from the burning blood.

Another blinding white flash and sparks fly from the

tree nearest Nana, forks of lightning making the entire tree glow yellow and orange and blue. Nana leans forward, over the altar, offering her blood to the fire.

And suddenly, things start to make sense to Sammy. Though she still screams, she can see where this is going. She somehow knows that the smoke coming from the blood will collect above the fire, as it is doing, and she knows what it will do next.

When Nana finally collapses behind the altar, the smoke from the blood, black and hanging like a cloud above the fire, begins to move. It swirls through the air, a spiral of black thread, and when it gets close to Sammy, it stops, changes shape. Looking like hand now, its fingers caress Sammy, moving up and down her body.

When it enters her nose and mouth, it tastes of mud and wood, of death and rebirth. She trembles as the smoke fully fills her lungs. It absorbs into her bloodstream, and the world tilts to the left and right, spins all the way around, and the laughter, the grunts and growls from the forest intensify, growing louder than the wind and thunder and rain. And then all of it turns black and silent.

* * *

She can see red. It's as though it is her first thought, her first experience ever. A flash of light, stronger than any ball of lightning, and her tiny, fragile mind is blown to pieces; a great and spinning ball of expanding light and energy.

She is flying through the vast nothingness, the fire of her rapidly growing thoughts leaving a trail of dust in its wake. The dust glows red, just like the beginning of this strange experience, but they quickly cool to yellows, greys and blues.

Steam. Water cooling on dark land with black clouds. And something is crawling from the black, watery muck. It is small, brown, gills along the sides of its neck. It almost looks human as it raises a fin that sort of looks like an arm to the sky. The sound it makes is high-pitched and makes the sky cry tears of sulphur.

Bones snap and crackle, and once more Sammy is awake, back in her suit of perception. She can see the light of the fire and though the rain has stopped, the grass beneath her face is cold and wet. Distant thunder and the laughter of demigods fill her ears, but she barely notices for the pain that racks her body. She opens her eyes and can actually see the bones in her arms and legs as they break and reform. Hair covers her entire body, and her dress is stretching, tearing at the seams with her growing arms.

Above, the moon is full, and shines down upon her. Her fear along with the confusion melt away.

You will find out who you are, Nana had said.

She reaches for the silver in the sky. Its beauty is overwhelming, causing the oceans within her very soul to shift. And she cries out, but it sounds more like laughter to her ears. Like howling.

And then she's running. Flying through the trees. None of the branches dare touch her with their skeletal fingers.

* * *

She awakes to rough hands pawing and petting the bare skin of her back. Sunlight streams through the trees in brilliant, golden beams. A mist blankets the surrounding forest. The fire looks as though it had died a long time ago, but still a line or two of smoke rises from its ashes.

Sammy turns around and looks up into the black beads

that are her grandmother's eyes. The old woman is smiling, her teeth yellow and brown in the sunlight. There's not even a trace of a wound on her neck.

"Wh ... What happened?" Sammy says. Her voice sounds different, deeper and stronger.

"You're now a woman," Nana says. "Your own mother would have been proud, had she not bothered with that damned church. But I'm proud of you."

Pain returns as Sammy sits up. It strikes at her sides as though someone had punched her there. She looks down, not surprised to see that the clothes she had worn last night are in shreds over her skin. She's nearly naked and is surprised, however, at the blood in the spot between her legs.

"You've gotten your first blood," Nana says. "You'll be very strong, should you ever decide to take the path of the Old Ones. You should have seen yourself last night. Magnificent. Beautiful. You were a goddess in your own right."

"I ... I've never felt so *alive!*" Sammy says, and she wants to jump up and laugh. She wants to again feel the moon on her skin while she runs, surrounded in its brilliance. But the pain in her sides, deep within her guts, makes her groan instead.

"You'll have plenty of time, child," Nana says, again reading her mind. "But you know what you are now, don't you?"

Sammy looks deep into the abyss that is her grandmother's eyes. She nods her head, wonders what her mother and father will think.

"Will you teach me?"

"I already am," Nana says, and laughs. "But for now, we should return. You go back home later today. It might be best if you don't tell your parents of what we did out here. At least for a while. Is that okay with you?"

"Are you kidding? I ... I don't think they'd get it."

Nana stands and reaches for the altar. From within it, she pulls out a plastic bag that's full of what looks like red, fluffy robes.

"Put this on before you catch your death, dear," Nana says, passing her a robe and a pair of slip-on shoes.

Once the robes are snug around their skin, Nana reaches out for Sammy. This time they hold hands as they head back into the woods. Toward home.

Divorce and the Black Cat

He stood outside in the dark, hoping for a glimpse of her. He swayed like a branch in the wind, but there was no wind, only the taste of cheap whiskey still on his tongue, drying his tongue with each inhalation. He needed another drink, but first he wanted to tell Nicole what he thought of her. It had been a long time coming, and she needed to *know*.

But would it stop there? Nick was afraid to find out. But he had come. Even if he didn't have total control over his actions or emotions, he had to do this. There was no other choice. The pain deep in his chest would not go away, no matter how much he drank.

The worst of it was that he feared he was going insane. He found himself doing things, mean things, even when he was sober. It was as though something else was taking over and letting him remain to watch everything he did. Just the other day, at the factory, he had cornered an eighteen-year-old know-it-all in the corner of the cafeteria when they were alone, threatening the boy with his pocket knife. The only thing the kid had done wrong was shoot his mouth off, like any other teenager, but this time, something had clicked inside Nick's skull, and he found himself threatening to cut the boy open from scrotum to chin if he didn't shut up.

The poor bastard quit the next day. Apparently, the kid no longer enjoyed working there.

Still, Nick worried. He'd never acted that way before. Not sober. He'd had the thoughts, sure, who hasn't? But he'd never gone through with any of them.

A light in the basement turned on, and Nick went to the small window close to the ground, crouched over. Inside and below was the pile of extra bricks he had used to fix the basement's walls. With it were the bags of mortar mix. Nicole came down the steps, stopping on the bottom step. She looked around before heading back up. Nick supposed that she was making sure that the new sub pump was still doing its job. She glared at the bricks and mortar mix, shook her head with a look of disgust on her face.

Rage blossomed in Nick's chest.

Now was the time. He'd never felt more confident, more sure of his convictions.

When he stood up a loud hiss startled him. He turned to find Pluto, his and Nicole's cat, looking at him. They had found the cat wandering around the community five or six years ago. They had posted signs but nobody came to claim the cat, so they decided to keep it themselves. Nick was hesitant at first because of an old wives tale his mother used to tell him, that black cats were really witches in disguise. Nicole was smarter than that, though.

"We'll call her Pluto," she had said. "Pluto is an ancient Pagan god all witches are afraid of."

Nick thought the logic behind this was stupid, but then his own paranoia was pretty silly, too. Yet, to his surprise, man and cat became good friends. Pluto would often sit on his lap while he watched baseball or hockey, letting him pet her belly while she purred like an engine. The cat liked him so much, in fact, that he thought that she must be part dog; she became excited when he got home from work, or the bar, rubbing her head up against his legs and meowing at him.

The cat hissed at him again. He got a good look at the crater within Pluto's skull where there used to be an eye.

One night he had come home drunk and must have startled her, because she had run away from him.

This was the first time the other presence had fully taken over control of his body. Rage filled him. How dare the cat run away from *him*?

He had chased Pluto, finally cornering her in the garage. He grabbed her by the scruff of the neck and held her at eye level. He would have left it there, but the cat hissed and took a swipe at his face.

He had watched himself, helplessly, as his pocket knife magically appeared in his hand, as he forced the cat, his former friend, up against the wall.

He watched himself as he gouged out its eye.

Thinking of this, the rage went away and Nick almost felt human again. Drunk, but human. Pluto sat on the flowerbed Nicole had placed upon the window ledge. She stared at him, her one eye glittering green and yellow. She growled a low, mean sound. Nick bent down, held his face close to hers. She retreated, her back arched.

"I'm sorry I hurt you," he said. "I didn't mean it."

Her paw slashed out, the nails extended and slicing through the skin of his cheek.

"Fucking bitch!" he said. The cat jumped off the flowerbed and ran into the back yard.

Nick touched his cheek. There was blood on his fingers when he pulled his hand back.

"Fucking bitch!" he repeated, and then he was in the passenger seat again, watching himself as he ran into the backyard after Pluto, his pocketknife in his hand, the blade withdrawn and reflecting the backyard's light.

Pluto tried scuttling up a tree, but Nick was too fast for it. She was halfway to the first branch when he snatched her by the scruff of the neck.

Pluto didn't have a chance to fight him off this time. The knife entered the feline's belly again and again and again until blood bubbled from its mouth and its intestines plopped with a sickening *thwak* on the ground below.

Nick took a step back and didn't realize that he had control over his actions again until he dropped the dead cat onto its own gore and clasped a bloody hand over his mouth.

What had he done?

And more important, if he was capable of this, of what else was he capable?

It was the demon-alcohol's fault. He knew it. But what was he to do?

He ran to the front of the house, jumped back into his small, rusted Toyota. He chugged deeply from the half-emptied bottle of Jack Daniels and drove back to his apartment across the city, the things he wanted to tell Nicole forgotten.

* * *

His first mistake was leaving an unopened bottle of Jack in the cupboard. Staying sober included emergencies, so there went that excuse. Perhaps he should have joined a twelve step program. At least he had made it a full month without even a sip.

In truth, he had never felt better for it. The sobriety had cleared his mind, and he wasn't so tired all the time. For the first fifteen days, he hadn't even tried to contact Nicole. She hadn't tried to contact him, either. Although he thought about her all the time, missed her like he would a limb, the pain and the sickness that came with it was so much easier to take. To control.

For the second fifteen days, he not only talked to her, but had shared coffee with her at a Tim Horton's. Neutral territory, as she had called it, felt much better than he had anticipated. He had expected awkward silences, accusations, tears. He had expected to hate sitting in some coffee shop while he slowly lost whatever control he had managed to gain.

Instead, they both laughed and discussed stupid, useless things. Movies, television. Bullshit.

He had then told her of his sobriety, and she changed the subject.

Nick looked at his dear old friend, Jack. Such a slick fellow he was. His liquid brown essence was nearly golden, though the bottle was half gone. Nick laughed and poured more into his cup. Being sober had killed his immunity. *Half-empty bottle and I'm fully in the bag*, he thought.

Beside the bottle was the pile of mail he had picked up before coming home. On top of the pile were the divorce papers Nicole's lawyer had sent him.

The bitch! The betraying bitch!

Yet he couldn't stop laughing. She had been so polite, so kind, and perhaps, or so he had thought, flirtatious the other day when they had coffee together. She had also seemed reserved about something. Perhaps she had planned on telling him about the divorce papers but chickened out? She had to have known what she was doing. But why pull this on him? And now?

She was sleeping with someone, and had been for a long time now. That was it. He just knew it.

His laughter died, and he realized that his vision was blurry with tears.

Was he laughing? Crying?

He couldn't remember. All he knew was that his throat and mouth were dry, and that his chest ached with the pain of the past couple of months. There seemed to be no end in sight.

He had to talk to her. He had to see her face. She had to know what was plaguing him. She had to take him back.

* * *

His second mistake was pocketing the knife he had used to kill Pluto with.

* * *

He nearly hit Nicole's car when he pulled into the driveway. He slammed on the brakes, the Toyota stopping inches away.

"You shouldn't drink and drive," he told the steering wheel. "Shhh, I won't tell anyone if you don't."

He lumbered out of the old Toyota and closed the door behind him. He was still holding dear old Jack in his hand, and he looked at it with surprise.

Nick looked to John Marster's driveway where, at the end, were garbage cans for tomorrow's pick up. Nick looked forward to getting back into silly schedules such as taking out the garbage. He craved being a husband again. Maybe one day he and Nicole could even have a kid. Nick thought about being a father, and smiled. He'd be a great father, he knew.

He found the house key and headed for the front door. Ignorant of the time, he unlocked the door and stepped inside. He closed it behind him, and when he turned back around, he jumped.

A black cat stood on top the wall partition separating

the front lobby from the living room, just as Pluto used to do when she wanted out.

The cat hissed at him and arched its back.

Swaying, Nick laughed and bent over for a closer look. The cat backed up and glared at him. It looked exactly like Pluto. It even had the same crater where an eye used to be. The only difference was that there was a white patch on its chest.

Nick wondered if his wife had found the corpse of Pluto in the backyard a month ago, and had decided to replace Pluto with this creature. Funny that she hadn't mentioned it the other day, but then she had failed to mention the divorce papers, too.

He looked closer at the cat's white patch. It almost looked … Yes, indeed, it *was* the silhouette of a knife. A fold-away pocketknife, just like his.

His eyebrows narrowed and he looked back into the cat's single eye.

"Pluto?"

The cat hissed, its paw shooting out at his cheek.

Nick screamed; his hand clasped against his cheek. When he pulled his hand away, it was streaked with blood. The little bitch had cut him! But when he looked for it, it was gone. It had jumped into the living room and stood on the couch, hissing at him.

"You little bitch," Nick said, jumping around the wall partition and into the living room. The cat howled and jumped onto the floor, scrambling to get under the couch. Nick was just in time to grab its back legs before it was totally gone, but a voice to his left stopped him.

"Nick, is that you?"

Nick turned, and there she was. His wife, or soon to be ex-wife. The love of his life. She was wearing only her slip, her sandy hair a mess. Her bloodshot eyes were wide, and she stood by the entrance to the kitchen. The kitchen light was on, and Nick wondered how long she had been standing there.

"N ... Nick, what are you doing here? It's nearly midnight."

"You've got a charming cat here," Nick said. He let go of the cat, stood up and took a step closer to her. She took a step back.

Fighting the rage, he said, "Where's Pluto?"

"That was Pluto."

Nick shook his head, nearly lost his balance.

"What are you doing here, Nick?" Nicole repeated. "It's nearly midnight, and I have to work in the morning. Wait a minute, are you *drunk*? I can't believe you came here drunk! Go home, Nick!"

Nick didn't move. He smiled, looked up at the ceiling.

"You know," he said, "I was totally sober for an entire month, and you didn't care. I mean, my drinking is the reason you kicked me out, right?"

Nicole didn't answer.

"Well, that's what you told me, anyway. I told you just the other day, when we had coffee together, but you just changed the subject." He paused. He could hear Nicole breathing.

"Funny how you didn't tell me about those divorce papers you were sending me."

"I wanted to," Nicole said, her voice small. "But I was afraid."

"I never told you how much I love you," Nick continued as though he hadn't heard her. "I know that was hard on you. But I do love you. I don't want to drink anymore, Nicole. I want to get help. I want us to get back together and work out our problems. Whatever it takes."

More silence, broken by the clunk of the sub pump turning on and off in the basement. Nick searched Nicole's eyes. They were wet with tears and she was hugging herself. She looked into the kitchen, her lips trembling.

For a moment, Nick thought that she'd run into his arms and tell him that she loved him. That she was glad this nightmare was over.

"I can't," she said. "I can't be with you anymore, Nick. I've already told you. I don't love you anymore."

"Who is it, then? Who're you fucking?"

"There's nobody else, Nick. I just don't want to be with you. Now get out!"

Nick blinked, and then the pocket knife was in his hands. How had that gotten there? He didn't remember grabbing it. But there it was, opened and reflecting the kitchen light. He could see Nicole reflected in there, too; thin and distorted.

Power flooded Nick, but he was no longer in control. The demon-alcohol had taken over, but this time Nick didn't mind sitting in the back seat. He knew he was in for a good time.

He watched himself take a step towards Nicole. He watched her retreat.

"Stop walking away from me!" he said, and then he was chasing her into the kitchen, past the stove and fridge and down the stairs into the basement. She was going for the garage entrance, he knew, but he was too quick for her and caught her at the bottom of the stairs. He tangled his foot between her feet and pushed her to the hard cement floor. She landed with an audible "Ummph!"

He turned her around so that she faced him and straddled her. The demon-alcohol wasted no time and Nick watched as the knife penetrated Nicole's neck and chest.

Soon she stopped struggling. Her eyes grew slack. Blood stained their clothes, their hands, her face and hair, the cold cement floor. She stared up, looking at nothing.

Nick stood and waited for the guilt, the dread that had followed after Pluto. He felt nothing, though. Sober, perhaps, intoxicated with power, most certainly. But now he had a job to do.

He looked at the brick and mortar on the other side of the room.

Looks like he'd be using the extras after all.

* * *

"So, when your wife went missing, why didn't you report it?"

"I thought she went to her mother's. She does that sometimes."

The cop smiled, as though he had just caught Nick in a lie. There were two of them, one nearly seven feet tall with blond hair, the other much shorter with black hair. They had introduced themselves as Constables Vanwrite (the tall blond) and Chaplin. They both looked at him with blank stares, their smiles not reaching their eyes. They both looked at him as they would a cockroach, and Nick was getting sick of it. He couldn't do anything about it. If they demanded to come into the house, it was probably game over.

He had known that they would come, but he didn't think they would have this early. It had been only four days, after all. And he wasn't the one to have phoned the cops to tell them that she was missing. Perhaps he should have, he thought. It would have made getting out of this much easier, especially considering the past few days had involved nothing but alcohol, hangovers, and work.

He wondered who had phoned the cops. Nick had un-plugged the phone days ago, it was ringing so much.

He stumbled and shook his head. *Try to look sober, you idiot!* he thought. But they could smell the whiskey off him like cologne. The way they had scrunched their noses up in repulsion when he had answered the door had told that tale well enough.

"Still," the tall one, Vanwrite, said. "You're coming with us. We have a few more questions to ask.

Nick put on his best smile. When he spoke, he tried his best to enunciate every word so as not to slur. "And why can't we do that here, officer? I'm sure that my couch and chair are more comfortable than wherever you want to go." *Shit*, he thought. *I can't have them inside!* "Or the porch here," he added.

"Don't make us arrest you," Chaplin said. This time the smile did reach his eyes.

"I bet you'd like to do that, wouldn't you? Maybe rough me up a little?" Nick took a step back. He hadn't meant to say that. It was too late to try and cover it up. He was suddenly on the floor, his hands behind his back, a knee pressed into his spine, right between the shoulder blades. He couldn't move, couldn't breathe.

"You fuck," Nick said, but it sounded more like a grunt. "I didn't do anything, you fuckers. Let me go!"

"Shut your mouth, Mr. Poulson, before you get yourself in more trouble."

A scream cut through the evening, loud and shrill, si-lencing both the cops and Nick. It had sounded as though it had come from *inside* the house. Silence followed, and although Nick couldn't see the cops, he knew they were looking in at the kitchen beyond the front door.

The scream came again, muffled but feminine, calling out for help.

"Holy shit, did you hear that?" Chaplin said.

"I heard it, all right," Vanwrite said.

"It's just the cat," Nick said. "You scared it."

Nick didn't realize until then that he hadn't seen the cat since the night it had scratched his face, before he killed Nicole. But that's what the scream had sounded like.

"Probable cause, Vanwrite?" Chaplin said.

"Oh, I think so."

They both grabbed an arm and hoisted Nick to his feet. He walked between them as they entered the kitchen. The scream came again, a wordless cacophony of agony. Nick's heart sank. The screams were coming from the basement.

Vanwrite let go of Nick's arm, pulled his gun and said, "Hold him," to Chaplin.

"He ain't goin' anywhere." The other man's grip was like steel, his hand hot against his skin.

Slowly, they went down the stairs, no one speaking. Nick wanted to pull away from Officer Chaplin and run, but that last scream had sounded like Nicole. She was dead. He had made sure of it. Nobody could survive what he had done to her. But he had heard her *scream*!

The screaming stopped once they reached the basement. Vanwrite and Chaplin exchanged frightened looks. Nick realized that his arms had sprouted an army of goose bumps, his breath misting before his eyes.

"Please..." a voice whispered. "H-H-Help me ..."

They turned the corner, and then there it was. The wall he had built just a few days ago. Only now, it wasn't simply red bricks and gray mortar. At the very center, there was the silhouette of a cat. And from the center came the weak, dying voice.

"... help me ..."

Vanwrite used his shoulder radio. "This is Constable

Vanwrite. I'm at one- eighteen Edgar Road. I need back up!" His voice trembled as he spoke, and when he was finished, he looked at Nick and let go of the shoulder radio.

"Time to see just what kind of sick shit you've got down here," he said. He searched around the basement while Chaplin cuffed him to a water pipe.

They settled on using some of the bricks that Nick hadn't used. They pounded at the wall, both their shoulder radios buzzing with activity as they worked. Chaplin found a hammer and used it. Within minutes, they had created a sizable hole, and were soon shining flashlights in.

Both men drew back quickly, covering their mouths. They gagged, cursed, and they looked at Nick with a new form of disgust. When they moved, he could see it all for himself. There was Nicole, the veins of her face having turned black, dried blood having turned brown, her eyes filmed over milky white.

Sitting on her shoulder was Pluto. She meowed a long, mournful cry and jumped through the hole onto the floor where she scampered away into the shadows.

Breathing hard, Nick stared at the body of his dead wife. She stared back, and then she blinked.

Nick screamed as she tilted her head up and the wall began to protrude outwards. He pointed with his free hand, but the cops were looking at him as though he had lost his mind. Perhaps he had, because they didn't even respond when the wall collapsed at their feet and Nicole was freed. She held in her hand the pocketknife he had used to kill her, but this no longer surprised him. It was the black cat, Pluto, he knew. A witch wearing the disguise of a cat had orchestrated all of this, his drunkenness, his insanity, his homicide. The screams he was hearing turned to the laughter of a mad man.

He laughed as Nicole raised the knife and swung it down into Vanwrite's neck. Blood spurted as she tore the knife through his trachea, then turned to Chaplin, who stood staring at her with wide eyes and a pale face. Nick laughed as she quickly closed the distance and slit his throat, too.

He laughed as she dug the keys out of the dying man's pocket, as she stumbled over to him, undid his cuffs, and then placed the pocketknife into his hand.

She smiled at his laughter, her breath cold and smelling of decay. She ran a finger down his check and said, "I loved you once." Then she collapsed. Lifeless. Dead.

Nick was still laughing when the backup Vanwrite had called arrived five minutes later.

House of Coal

All Jackson remembers from last night is panic. He recalls only parts of the trip home from work, and then the fury, the painful beating of his heart as he had pulled into his driveway. He remembers running to the neighbor to find a telephone, and the tears that had dripped tar-black down his smoke-colored cheeks. Now, everything smells like the smoke, the greasy powder that had fallen from the walls and ceiling of his home to land and embrace everything in its path. Everything ruined and Kingsley, the fire chief, inside right now, wandering through the rubble, inspecting the cause. "Looks like something near the fridge," he had said only moments ago, before heading in for a second or third look. "Did you have anything flammable sitting anywhere near it?"

"No," Jackson had said. Now he feels exhausted, worn out, the sun beginning to rise and bleed purple into the sky. Birds chirp in the trees surrounding him, but none of this everyday crap matters. Only the pungent stench of smoke and the fire chief inside his house, rooting through his things and him standing outside alone. The ambulances, the fire trucks and police cruisers had left not long ago, but Jackson remained behind to answer repeated questions, stand around and watch nosy neighbors watch him. It should have been him, the color of charcoal. He should have at least been there with them, because now every-thing is gone. He realizes that he is still wearing the blan-ket a police officer had offered earlier while questioning him to help the chill that had nestled deep inside his bones. The kind of chill that digs deep into your body and never truly goes away. Death in the next faded heart beat. *If only … if only …*

"Yup, definitely started somewhere behind the fridge," the voice of the fire chief comes from behind, startling Jackson.

"I believe the fire started inside the wall. The house is old. Faulty wire, maybe. Do you know when the house was last rewired?"

"We bought it only a few years ago," Jackson says. "I have no idea."

"The former home-owners never mentioned anything?"

"They were an old couple. Died one after the other. If there is any kind of information like that, it'll be upstairs in the bottom drawer of the dresser along with the rest of the paper work."

"Great, I'll get to that as soon as I can. Now, I have to ask that you stay out of the house until the inspector comes. The air inside is toxic, so I wouldn't advise it any-ways."

"Do you suspect arson?"

Kingsley pulls back his head and frowns. "No, if I did the police would still be here. Like I said, it looks as though it started inside the wall, but I'm not the expert here. The official inspector will confirm it." The fire chief pauses, as though realizing something. More birds chirp in the trees, the congregation singing a lament. "You should've left with your family," the fire chief says. "Looks like you should see a doctor, though. Tell ya what, I'll contact the insurance company for you. We'll hook up later when you're feeling better." Again he pauses, then adds, "I'm sorry for your loss," as though these words alone could fill the sudden hole inside him, could heal the wound that only feels physical but is not and might never stop bleeding. The sting of tears fills Jackson's eyes, and although his mouth is opening and closing, like a fish, no words come out. And when the words do come out of Jackson's mouth, they are mutilated and choked.

"They're all gone," he says, the watery tar-black dripping all the way down to his chin. He looks away from Kingsley to the now hollow house. Hollowed of its soul and life and Jackson wants to go in there and lick the walls, taste the aftermath of death until he chokes on it.

"They're all dead."

The fire chief puts his hand on Jackson's shoulder. "It'll get easier with time," he says, but Jackson barely hears. "Let me get my truck, I'll take you to the hospital myself. You're in no shape to drive." Then he's gone, his bulk dissolving and Jackson is staring at the kitchen window. Just beyond the broken glass panel, there is a set of shadowy shoulders, a shadowy head with no hair and midnight slick skin. The whites of its eyes blink, and a two rows of large teeth catch the sun and begin to chatter with loud ticking sounds.

Jackson tries to scream, but the world around him closes in, and he can feel the ground coming up to greet his body as everything, the neighbors watching from porches and windows, the chirping birds and the blinding sun disappear and go blessedly silent.

* * *

Two hours later and Jackson is still unconscious. Dreams do not leave him alone. He is standing in his home, the way it was only one day ago. In the living room, all is silent, the soft orange light from the lamp and a blue florescent glow from the television illuminate the room, and Jackson, in the middle of the room, feels relaxed. Adel and Jesse and Otto are in the other rooms, tucked peacefully inside their beds. Jackson knows this, and tries to call out to them, but they cannot hear him, so he tries to move, to go to them, but his limbs are heavy, lethargic and limp. With an audible *tink*, the sound of a blown light bulb, the living room fades to pitch-black.   The muscles in his legs stiffen and cramp, but still he cannot move.

Silver light fills the blackness, the moon moving faster than it does in real time, fills the window behind him.

Shadows move within the inky blackness, silver moon rays catching the whites of their eyes. Jackson can move again, and he raises his arms, stretches them out before him, his fingers reaching for the things out there. The smell of smoke clogs the inside of his nostrils, and his fingers graze upon one of the hairless creatures moving, dancing around him. Its skin is like touching scorched wood and its flesh chips to ash and charcoal-black paints his fingers. He pulls back and expects retaliation, but none comes, the creature he had touched converges in with the rest, their teeth and eyes blocked only by the crazy movement of their arms. *The people of death, the people of coal*, and the smoke trails into the living room, exciting the creatures, the sound of snapping fingers and the fire climbs the wall just inside the next room, in the kitchen, and its almost comforting glow of campfire yellow and orange illuminates the entrance.

The smoke collects around the dancing tribesmen, fills their essence and their eyes grow, their teeth expanding to the size of wooden planks and only get bigger. As they close in, their scorched wooden fingers and tongues dig into his nose, into his mouth, down his throat and *Coal to soak in all the poison*. The words fill his ears; they silence the snap and crackle of the fire consuming his life. He tries to scream, but he is suffocating in their embrace, their teeth white and large, so large that it's all he can see. He blinks the tears away from his eyes, the light, fluorescent now and horribly white, blinds and stings, digs deep into his eyes like daggers. There is an external gasp, a quick breath of air, then "Chief Kingsley, I think he's awake now," and the chief's large shoulders and head eclipse the fluorescents.

"Had us all worried there for a while, little buddy," he says and smiles. Jackson winces at the man's large teeth. "I had to call another ambulance after you took that nose dive." Cold fingers press against his wrist, and Jackson realizes a nurse is standing to his left, checking his pulse. She too smiles, melancholic but well meaning. When she's done she writes something down on her clipboard, then leaves. Her sneakers squeak upon the waxed floor. As Jackson sits up, rubbing his eyes to try to clear them, the world tilts with vertigo and nausea. In front of his bed, there are white walls with grey bordering and three metal tiers full of intravenous bags, plastic hypodermics, Popsicle sticks and wound dressings. He concentrates on these for a moment, to fight the nausea, and expects the scent of hospital, but all he can smell is the smoke from the fire. He looks down to see that he's still wearing the same clothes from last night, all streaked in black from that one moment he went inside the smoke congested house and called out to Adel, to Otto and Jesse, but with no answer. The sound of crackling fire had been layered over a dreadful silence, a silence he'll never forget.

The fire chief steps in front of the bed, blocking the view of the white wall and the supply shelf. His smile is gone, and his eyes hold pain that is foreign to the man's previous disposition. "I'm really sorry about your family," he says. "And I'm also sorry if I seemed unsympathetic earlier this morning. I just never know the right thing to say to people who've lost so much."

How about just shutting the fuck up and leaving me alone. The thought is not a question, but a desperate demand. Jackson keeps the words to himself. "Is there any reason you're still here?" he asks. The fire chief raises his eyebrows again, two thick caterpillars climbing his forehead, and for reasons lost to Jackson, the man looks surprised.

"Just worried about you. Besides, I wasn't here the whole time. I just came back about ten minutes before you woke to check up."

"Well, I'm still alive, thank you. So if you don't mind, I'd like to be alone and wait for the doctor release me."

Chief Kingsley nods his head, purses his thin lips.

"Unless, of course, you have more questions?"

"No, but I do have some news from your insurance. They're sending out an adjuster. He'll be around the site sometime this afternoon to assess some of the damage. He'll want to get a statement from you."

"Do I have to be there today?"

"No, considering the circumstances. So tell me, where you gonna stay? Family? Friends?"

Jackson frowns, his only possessions, aside from his car, are smoky and black underneath the hospital's clean sheets. "No," he says. "I'm all alone now."

"Not even an aunt or uncle somewhere?"

Why won't this bastard just leave me alone? "Yeah, but they live in Montreal and Edmonton."

Chief Kingsley nods his head again as though taking a second to register the information.   "You can stay with me, if you want. I got an extra room, and Maggie won't mind."

"If it's all the same to you, Chief, I'll do fine just getting a room somewhere until I can find a place of my own."

"Just offering," the chief says. "If you change your mind, you know where to get a hold of me."

He turns and steps out of the room, and Jackson is finally alone. He shifts position on the bed, wonders how he's going to get home, or *where* he's going to go for that matter. As the uncertainty cultivates inside his stomach, spreading its dark wings up into the sensitive parts of his ribcage, he realizes that he truly does not want this isolation. He craves the company of those who can no longer comfort him, take care of him, the ones who could foster this sudden loneliness and make him feel complete and in control.

* * *

The motel room is small, but it's all Jackson can afford. The bathroom is such that when you sit on the toilet your knees rub against the minute vanity, and if you stand before the mirror and turn too quickly, you run the risk of falling into the bathtub. The kitchen is the size of a broom closet holding a miniature sink, small counter, two electric burners, and a bar fridge. The bedroom and living space is the biggest room with a double-sized bed and the Seventeen-inch television Jackson is sitting in front of on an uncomfortable chair that looks decades old.

He is wearing the cheap Wal-Mart suit fellow bartenders had helped him buy with their kindly donations and a tip-jar over at the bar with a sign on it saying, "Help our fellow, who lost everything, get back on his feet." Below the words, there was a picture of Jackson serving drinks.

News travels fast in this town. The day after the fire, after Jackson had called his boss telling him of the tragedy and that he needed a few days off, people he barely knew stopped him on the street to offer condolences they did not really mean, just doing it for the sake of fuzzy warm feelings. His boss had passed him a few envelopes full of fives, tens, twenties, and one with a roll of quarters. And the clothes; Jackson probably has more clothing now than ever before.

But dreams of the hairless creatures, painted midnight-black with smoke grease, their flesh of charcoal and scorched wood, do not leave him alone. Jackson can see them when he is awake, while talking with the insurance adjuster, driving the car, and even today, in the cemetery near the end of his family's funeral. Always in the shadows, hiding behind trees, inside other people's homes and cars and staring out at him through windows, their teeth long and white, their eyes large circles of hunger and lust.

Sitting on the chair, smoking a cigarette, Jackson feels nothing. A great humming silence deep in his core and until now the cigarettes a habit avoided. Yet, when he puts the cigarette up to his lips and pulls hard, inhaling the grey smoke, his head feels feather-light, his vision blurs. He stays close to the element that had consumed his life, suffocated his family, smoking one cigarette after another, not minding the subsequent vomiting or the sleepless nights. He sits with his arms flat on the armrests. In his other hand, a bottle of bourbon scotch. His eyes red-rimmed and half-open, lips parted. A new age zombie wearing a suit and tie. The television on, but nobody to pay it any attention.

A knock on the door, Jackson jumps, and the long shaft of disregarded ash drops from the burning ember of the cigarette and crumbles to the floor. Another knock, more desperate than the one snapping Jackson back into real time, real life, and "Jackson, are you in there, buddy? Come on, answer the door."

Jackson snubs the cigarette into the ashtray sitting on the nightstand, lights another, gets up and answers the door. He expects family visiting from other provinces for the funeral, his mother or father, his in-laws, but it's Chief Kingsley standing there, knuckles poised to knock again. "Boy you look like shit! Look even worse than earlier this afternoon at the funeral." He waves his hand in front of him, left to right, left to right. "And you stink. What's that shit you got there, whiskey?"

Jackson's mind crawls back to that other place, where dreams and reality are almost one, and he cannot digest everything the chief has said. So he says, "What do you want?" instead, avoiding Chief Kingsley's worried and sus-picious eyes, the flush in his cheeks spreading as though the man is embarrassed for Jackson, feels sorry for the pa-thetic piece of shit before him. Jackson looks down at his feet.

"I came to see how you're holding up, and now that I've seen you, I think that it's time for you to stop feeling sorry for yourself. Come on, let's go for some coffee and sober you up."

Jackson looks up into the chief's eyes, can feel blood heat-ing his own face now, and white spots fill his vision. Who is this man to judge him? A man he didn't even know a week ago. And now he's staring at Jackson like a long lost friend, his expression full of sympathy and the *I'm gonna take care of you whether you like it or not* hard love. "I don't want any coffee," Jackson says. "I just want to be left alone." And he goes to close the door in Kingsley's face, but the fat man is too quick, sticking his foot into the door, and he says, "I know what's happening to you. And if you stay in this state, you will die."

The door bounces off the chief's foot, and Jackson lets it open again. He says, "What if that's what I want?"

"I wouldn't blame you," Kingsley says. "But not like this. Come for coffee with me. We have to talk."

A dull, throbbing pain behind Jackson's eyes, his body dehydrating, and perhaps coffee is a good idea. "Talk about what?"

"The things you've been seeing since the fire," the chief says. "And what now lives inside your house."

* * *

The sun sinks eastward and there is a cold breeze blowing brown and yellow leaves down the street. The leaves fill the sky whenever wind blows strong enough to shake their former homes free of the dying to prepare for the long sleep. They fall to the ground and the wind swipes them up again, twirling them around in circles like lost souls, like baby birds thrust out of the nest too early. The dull pulse of voices in the café pulls Jackson back, and he looks away from the window, wonders why he never watched, sat down and really watched the artistic ritual of nature. Always too busy falling to the rituals of life, avoiding the inevitable as though it were something you could hide from, autumn and winter, old age and death.

"Here we go," Kingsley says, sitting down across from Jackson and placing a bottle of water and a coffee in front of him. "Drink up, the water is so you don't dehydrate. The coffee can actually make you worse." Along with the coffee and water, Kingsley has also bought a sandwich. He picks it up off the plate, groans so that Jackson can almost see the man salivate, and digs in his large white teeth. A loud lettuce crunch and juice flows down his chin. He licks his lips once the bread and meat is away. Tiny crumbs hang onto his tongue and Jackson feels sick to his stomach. Feels as though the half-pint of whiskey he drank in under an hour is just sitting there, on the upper level of his stomach like sour milk, and he wonders if he'll have to sit and watch Kingsley eat. He turns his head and looks out the window, but something tar-black catches the corner of his eye.

"I hear we're in for a nasty winter," Kingsley says, and just behind him, shadows come alive. Behind another cos-tumer, on the other side of the room, slick black arms stretch out, the skin scaly like a snake, its bulbous head without hair, eyes, a nose, a mouth. It stretches up and turns around, places its hands upon the wall and begins to climb. Kingsley and everyone else in the café do not no-tice, the hum of many conversations continue to pulsate in Jackson's eardrums, and no one in the long line-up even flinches as the naked creature climbs the wall, leaving dark, oily hand and foot prints as it goes. "A long cold win-ter," Kingsley says and Jackson tries to pretend nothing is wrong. "Lots of snow, and a lot of really cold days." Kings-ley looks out the window, looks up to the sky overcast with low, threatening clouds. "Looks like it could snow any day now."

The creature reaches the top, crawls on its hands and knees across the ceiling, towards Jackson and Kingsley, its round head twirling around as though working out a cramp. *This isn't real*, Jackson thinks, *only in my head, this isn't real*, and aloud "I hate winter," hoping Kingsley hasn't noticed the sweat on his forehead, the shaking of his hands or the tremble in his voice. But Kingsley doesn't even look up, too caught up with his meaty sandwich and its finger licking juices to notice the thing almost above, its head thrashing, coiling, large teeth breaking through the mouth, thick black flakes falling from the crumbling fissure there, and it sounds like something chewing through wood or plaster.

"Can't say I'm a big fan of winter, either," Kingsley says. He must have looked up from his sandwich, because now he's reaching across the table. "Hey, buddy. You okay?" His hand touches Jackson's shoulder. Jackson flinches, and the thing above has stopped crawling. It opens its mouth wide, a sick and wretched smile, a howl of victory. Jackson's heart pounds painfully inside his chest. He can smell smoke; it fills his nostrils and makes it hard to breath. *"Chitta bit,"* the thing making noises through its mouth as its teeth gnaw and chew on nothing but air. *"Chitta dow,"* and Kingsley takes his hand away as Jackson heaves, then stands up quickly, the backs of his knees thrusting the chair away.

The murmur of voices stop, and everyone stares at Jackson, anxious eyes all over him, waiting for him to lose it. Some even appear to anticipate it, their mouths working up and down, "yes, yes, yes," old women and men with nothing better to do than watch television and gossip. Kingsley stares up at him, his eyes huge and worried. "Jackson?" he says. "What's wrong?"

"Chitta bit! Chitta dow!"

"I have to go," Jackson says clutching his stomach and looking at the floor as he rushes outside. He barely makes it before the vomit burns the back of his throat and he is puking on the café's front step, chasing away a young couple who had just pulled in. He rests his arm on the plastic garbage bin, the garbage inside overflowing with paper cups and uneaten donuts, the sweet smell of rot with flies buzzing. Jackson bends over and vomits until his stomach is empty. The sidewalk, littered with cracks that have tiny

blades of grass seeping through. The brick wall has cigarette butts sticking out of the mortar. The faces of Adel,
her premature grey hair, and little Otto and Jesse flash behind his eyelids when he closes his eyes. Their eyes unforgiving, digging holes into his mind, and when the retching
subsides, he sits down on the concrete, cool and wet from
his vomit.

He could die here, alone and detached from the world.

"Yeah, you could die here, if you really wanted." Jackson opens his eyes to Kingsley standing above him, reading
his thoughts as though he were an open book. "Here, you
forgot your coffee," Kingsley says, handing him the paper
cup. The coffee feels warm in his hands, sends chills to
race up his arms and dance upon his spine. He doesn't
open it, just holds it with both hands, hugging it close.

"I'm not used to this kind of pain," Jackson says. Kingsley sits down beside him, avoiding the vomit, and listens. "I
don't know what to do. A week ago, my life was normal,
always had been normal. We moved here about three
years ago because Adel was offered a good teaching job. I
knew I could find work here so I didn't mind. As a bartend-
er, I have seen all kinds of sorrow. I've seen a lot of loss,
people talk when they drink, you know? But I never
thought ..."

"Never thought it would happen to you," Kingsley fin-
ishes for him.

"Yeah," Jackson says. "And now I feel like ... I don't
know."

"You're different now," the chief says. "You can see
things now that most people can't, things that most people will go on and on in life and never see."

"And what does that make me, fucking special or something? I don't want to see the things I see!"

"It *makes* you different," Kingsley says, sounding irritated. "And that's all. You have a new life ahead of you now. You will never be the same, and eventually you will come to learn that. What will make you special is how you come through. On your hands and knees, bleeding from your stomach, or standing strong. The choice is up to you."

The fire chief stands up, brushes his pants free of dust and cold. "Well, I should get going now. Maggie will be waiting for me at home."

As he walks away, Jackson looks up and says, "You can see them too."

Kingsley turns around, a small smile plays at the corner of his lips, yet the smile does not reach his melancholic eyes. "Oh, I've seen 'them' since I was a kid, Jackson," he says. "And many worse things."

"Then what do I do?"

The wind teases the few hairs remaining on Kingsley's head. "You do what your gut tells you to do to survive, Jackson. That's all any of us can do."

* * *

Jackson stands in front of the ruined house.

Days have gone by, weeks, and Jackson has not see Kingsley. The man's words and what he might know work on Jackson's mind, but soon Jackson begins to forget where the wisdom even came from. He lives on instinct. He goes to work, returns to the motel and avoids the bottle. He takes care of himself, washing everyday and brushing his teeth, all the things a normal person should do. The restoration people are cleaning out the rubble and ruined furniture of the old house, preparing to rebuild. Jackson isn't sure if he wants to move back. Might sell the place and move back to the city. Back home. But something in his gut, his instincts, keeps him here, in this small town, everyday.

Perhaps he remains for the memory of his children, Otto and Jesse. The playgrounds, the school, and all the other kids they played with a monument. Perhaps he stays because this town is where Adel felt most happy, most at peace with herself. More likely, it has something to do with the bald men and women he sees climbing trees and walls while gnashing their teeth, their tar-black skin reflecting the light of the sun or moon, their eyes, when they have eyes, wild and insane. And the night, his time of work, has come alive in ways Jackson has never noticed before. He watches the streets from the window of his motel room. Before and after work, his eyes on the stars above, the slow ascent and descent of the moon, and the drunk, stoned children of the night, the ruined, starved souls, starved for an end to ritual and malevolence yet creating wickedness themselves with their mouths and fists. Flashing police lights, the cacophony of sirens and radios, and the snapping of handcuffs create more entertainment than the cable television his room came with. Reality is the true guts and grit of life.

Sometimes after work, he heads out for late-night walks, often passing the ruins of his life. He stands there now. The structure gloomy, enshrouded with shadows and it reminds Jackson of ghosts. In the back yard, the people of coal dance in circles around a bonfire under the stars. Jackson tries to talk to them, but they don't answer. They just move their bodies, snap their teeth at the cold, and so he stands with his hands in his pockets, the cool autumn night air biting at his cheeks. Since the incident, he's only been inside the house twice, once with the insurance adjuster, and a second time with the restoration crew. He avoids the place during the day. The sunlight no longer belongs in his realm of existence, the night marking the time of his rebirth.

You are different now. You have a new life ahead of you.

There is movement deep in the shadows of blackened windows. The early morning dancers are gone. They are waiting for him inside, have been since the first day he saw them. But they are patient in their waiting, would wait until the day Jackson died if they had to. He takes a step onto the property, steps past the large garbage bin, and wanders his way to the back door.

* * *

Inside, the house is silent, the same dreadful silence he experienced the night he opened the door and heard only the snap and crackle of fire. The smell of smoke is still strong, so strong that Jackson pauses a moment to cough. When his lungs finally begin to accept the air, he peels off his jacket and lets it fall onto the floor. Nowhere else to put it, the restoration people had taken most of the salvageable wooden furniture, leaving behind anything completely upholstered, completely ruined for the garbage. He curses himself for not bringing a flashlight, but his eyes are adjusting to the dismal light coming in through smoke-stained windows. He steps into the kitchen, where the fire had begun, and says, "Okay, here I am." Nothing answers, the room quiet and motionless.

Jackson kicks off his shoes and removes his socks. His feet make sucking sounds as he steps around. He feels the softness of the tiled floor, the grit from the walls and the part of the ceiling that had caved in. Next, he peels off his shirt, lets it fall to the blackened floor, and steps over to where the fridge used to be. The fridge stands near the middle of the room now so that the inspector could do his work. Jackson steps up to the wall, stares into the holes there, their depth, their darkness and complexity. He reaches out, touches the edge. *This one hole, this is where it started.* He knows this because the insurance adjuster had showed him when they went through the contents of the house. He also knows this because it feels right. The air inside the hole is cold and heavy, waiting to touch his warm flesh.

Jackson pulls his hand away to look at the black grease painted on his fingers. An oily residue that reminds him of hash oil he used to smoke back in school, before he met Adel. It too is cold on his cheeks as he rubs it in, painting his face black. He digs into the hole until his hands are as black as the environment around him. He paints his body the color of pain, the color of life cut short, the color of false security and everyday lies. A shade with all existing colors mixed in, the universe and everything now upon his chest and neck and face, and he bends over to remove his pants, his underwear, rubs the smoke onto his erection, beneath his balls, inside the crack of his ass, his legs and his feet, until he is completely covered. Until he can taste nothing but the smoke and it burns his lungs and makes him want to gag.

But he doesn't. Absolute animal instinct now and he fondles himself, calls out the names of his lost ones. "Adel," he says. "Otto, Jesse," and strokes himself up and down, up and down until his heart begins to race and the wall before him shifts, growing arms and opening eyes. Teeth as large as fingers smiling at him through that hole, urging him onward, and he wonders for a moment what Chief Kingsley would think of this madness if he were to see it. But the arms and legs stretch out, ending all thought, and he grips himself tighter as the limbs wrap around his body, pulling him inside, marking him as its next victim. He climaxes as his body touches the skeletal remains, and the pressure of being dragged into the wall does not hurt. Doesn't hurt because his body is liquefying with the orgasm, letting him pass between ribbed wooden beams like water, and the teeth are smiling. They smile and take Jackson in, and the world sinks, whirlpools down and down until there is nothing more.

* * *

Outside the burnt house, Jackson lights a cigarette. The taste fills his mouth, a disgusting taste that kept him from smoking throughout his adolescent days, but he enjoys the habit now. Even enjoys the taste. Somehow, it feels like home.

Running a hand through his hair thick with the stench of house fire, he takes a deep drag, and turns to head back to the motel. Behind, he leaves a trail of blue-grey mist in rhythm to his breath. The smoke raises into swirling, ghostly fingers, and the road ahead a labyrinth of murky streets, many sharp turns and a few dead ends. But the sky is turning a deep purple with the sun lurking just below the horizon, and Jackson shivers slightly in the early morning chill. It's the kind of shiver he knows will never entirely fade, but the thought doesn't bother him anymore. Winter is still far away.

Jason White has 15 short stories published with various venues, including both online and print magazines and anthologies. He lives and works in Central Ontario with his long time girlfriend. You can reach him online at www.jasonwhitefiction.com.

www.ingramcontent.com/pod-product-compliance
Lightning Source LLC
Chambersburg PA
CBHW071517170626
46811CB00007B/2885